This igloo book belongs to:

....

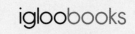

Published in 2016
by Igloo Books Ltd
Cottage Farm
Sywell
Northants
NN6 0BJ
www.igloobooks.com

HUN001 0916
3 5 7 9 10 8 6 4 2
ISBN: 978-1-78557-879-3

Printed and manufactured in China

Princess Stories

igloobooks

Contents

Stories for Younger Girls

....

Stories for Older Girls

....

Cinderella

Once upon a time, in a faraway kingdom lived, a beautiful young girl whose mother had died. Her father wanted to find her a new mother—so he married a widow. But the widow had two daughters of her own. She didn't want a stepdaughter, and saved all her love for her own children. She spoiled them with gifts and jewels.

For her husband's daughter, there was nothing. No pretty dresses, no sparkling necklaces, no loving hugs. Her new stepmother treated her like a servant, and made her work all day long. Only when evening came did she allow her stepdaughter to rest by the fire—though she made her sit among the ashes and cinders.

"Look at Cinder-ella!" her silly stepsisters would giggle. "Don't let her touch you! She's filthy! Just look at her feet!"

Of course, the name stayed with her. Soon everyone—even her father—called her Cinderella.

Life was hard for poor Cinderella, but she always tried to be cheerful.
"I have a father who loves me," she told herself whenever she felt sad. But Cinderella dreamed that one day she would find real happiness.

One morning, there was a knock at the door. Cinderella opened it to find a footman from the royal palace on the doorstep. He handed Cinderella an important looking envelope edged with gold.
"This is an invitation to the Prince's Birthday Ball tonight," he announced. "Every young maid in the land is invited."
"Give that to US!" cried the stepsisters, rudely snatching the envelope. "It's not for you!"
"The footman said every young maid is invited," said Cinderella, bravely.
Her stepmother smiled cruelly. She knew the Prince was looking for a wife. She also knew that Cinderella was far more beautiful than her own daughters. The Prince would never choose to marry one of them if Cinderella was around. So she came up with a wicked plan.

7

"You may go to the ball," she told Cinderella. "If you finish all your jobs." The two stepsisters sniggered. "Goodness! There's so much to do! You must wash and iron our dresses, polish our shoes, make our lunch, curl our hair, trim our nails, and order the coach." It would be impossible to finish in time! All day long, Cinderella washed and ironed, fetched and carried, as her cruel stepmother gave her more and more jobs to do. By the time her stepsisters were ready for the ball that evening, Cinderella was exhausted.

"Our coach is leaving right now," said her stepmother, unkindly. "What a shame you won't have time to get dressed and come, too."

Cinderella was disappointed–but she was determined not to let anyone see.

"Have a wonderful time," she called, waving good-bye.

As the coach drove away, a tear rolled down Cinderella's cheek. She longed to wear a beautiful gown, to twirl around the palace ballroom, to catch a glimpse of the handsome Prince!

"I wish I could go to the ball," she sighed, as she sat on her stool by the fire.

"And so you shall," said a voice, like tinkling music. Suddenly the room was filled with light. Cinderella looked up. There before her was a beautiful woman with rose-pink hair and the kindest eyes she had ever seen.

"I am your Fairy Godmother," said the woman gently. "Dry your eyes, my dear. We have work to do!"

"But how can I go to the ball?" exclaimed Cinderella.

"With the help of a little fairy dust, a pumpkin, six white mice and two rats," laughed her Fairy Godmother. "Now, bring them to me quickly."

Cinderella did as she was asked.

The Fairy Godmother placed the pumpkin on the ground and waved her wand over it. In a magical flurry of stars, it transformed into a stunning golden coach.

"And now for the horses and footmen," she cried, waving her wand once again. In an instant, six white horses appeared, and two handsome footmen.

Then the Fairy Godmother turned to Cinderella. "That dress will never do!" she said. Swoosh! She waved her wand one last time. Cinderella looked down and gasped. She was wearing a silk ball gown, encrusted with tiny pearls. It was exquisite! On her feet were two dainty glass slippers.

"I must be dreaming!" cried Cinderella, as a footman helped her up into the golden coach.

"It's not a dream," warned the Fairy Godmother, "but, like a dream, it can't last forever. At the stroke of midnight my magic will end. Everything you see before you will disappear."

"Don't worry! I won't forget," promised Cinderella, as her coach set off.

When Cinderella arrived at the ball, a murmur rippled through the room. "Who is that beautiful girl? She looks like an angel!" whispered the other guests as she stepped onto the dance floor. Even Cinderella's own stepsisters and stepmother didn't know who she was.

The Prince asked her to dance at once. He could not take his eyes off her, and refused to dance with anyone else. All night long, the young couple twirled around the dance floor beneath the twinkling chandeliers. It was clear to everyone the Prince had found the girl of his dreams.

At that very moment, the clock began to strike midnight. Cinderella remembered her Fairy Godmother's warning. The magic was about to end! "Oh no!" she cried, slipping from the Prince's arms and fleeing from the ballroom. As she rushed down the palace steps, Cinderella lost a glass slipper, but there was no time to stop.

The Prince raced after her. "Wait!" he cried. "Come back! I don't even know your name!"

But the beautiful girl in the pink dress had vanished. Only a dainty glass slipper remained, twinkling in the moonlight.

By now the Prince was in love with Cinderella.

"Go and search everywhere," he said to his ministers, picking up the slipper. "I cannot rest until she is found."

So, the next morning the Prince's ministers set out to try the glass slipper on every girl in the land. But not one could fit her foot into the tiny shoe.

Finally, the ministers arrived at Cinderella's home. Of course, the two stepsisters were determined that the glass slipper would fit them. They squeezed and pulled and pushed until they were red in the face—but they couldn't force their feet into the dainty slipper.

"Is there no one else?" asked the Prince, catching sight of a young girl watching through the banisters. It was Cinderella.

"She's just a servant, your Royal Highness," said her stepmother. "She didn't even go to the ball."

But the Prince would not be put off. There was something about the girl's fresh face and gentle manner that made his heart flutter. "Every young girl in the land must try it on," he ordered.

Cinderella held out her foot for the slipper, and the Prince slipped it on.

"It fits!" he cried in joy. "The slipper fits!"

In an instant, the room was filled with bright light, and the Fairy Godmother appeared.

With a wave of her wand, Cinderella's ragged dress was transformed
into a stunning bridal gown.

The Prince took her hands in his. "It really is you," he whispered. "I will never
let you go again."

Cinderella and the Prince were married the very next day. At last Cinderella's
dream for real happiness had come true!

The Princess Puzzle

Once upon a time, there was a splendid palace where a Princess lived with her parents, the King and Queen. The Princess was a beautiful, happy child, and on her next birthday she would inherit the palace and rule the kingdom.

In the days before the Princess's birthday, the palace was buzzing with activity. A huge party had been planned, and servants were rushing around the grand ballroom, cleaning, polishing, and hanging beautiful decorations. The party was very important, so no expense was spared. All the people in the kingdom were excited.

Everyone was so busy that they didn't notice the evil sorcerer outside the palace, peering through a window.

"That Princess shall not rule this land," the sorcerer hissed. "I want the kingdom for myself!"

The sorcerer drew a wand from his pocket and muttered a magical spell.

"Magicadabra and magicazane, magic two Princesses exactly the same!"

There was a loud BANG and a spray of pink sparks, followed by a puff of smoke. As the smoke cleared, a sly sneer crossed the sorcerer's face. He'd used his magic to create two girls who looked exactly like the Princess! The sorcerer laughed an evil laugh. Now there was no way the kingdom could be passed down to the Princess, because the King and Queen would never know who their real daughter was.

Later that day, the King and Queen called for their daughter. They couldn't

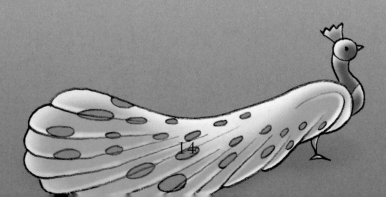

14

believe their eyes when three identical Princesses came running up to them! The girls all had tumbling dark locks, big hazel eyes, and porcelain skin. They could have been triplets.

"I'm your daughter," the first Princess said.

"Don't listen to her. I'm your daughter," the second Princess said.

"They're both lying, I'm your daughter," the third Princess pleaded, for she was the only one speaking the truth.

As the King and Queen stared at the girls closely, they were baffled. There was no way of knowing which of the Princesses were lying.

"How will we ever be able to tell who our daughter is?" the Queen asked, sadly.

"I have an idea," said the King. "I will set a series of tasks for them to complete. They will prove to us who the rightful Princess is."

The King called the Princesses, who lined up in front of his throne.

"Because it is impossible to tell you apart just by looking, I'm going to ask you to complete some tasks to help us decide which of you is our daughter," the King explained. "First of all, you must find an object only a Princess would know about."

The first Princess searched throughout the land and, in a cave at the top of a hill, she found a rare dragon's egg. She smiled with satisfaction, convinced that only a true Princess would be able to get such a thing.

The second Princess carefully hunted throughout the kingdom's forests and eventually found a precious curl of unicorn hair. She was sure the King would know only a true Princess could identify such an item.

The third Princess began her search, but hadn't been looking for long when she saw a little boy, alone and crying. She spent many hours helping the child find his parents and, by the time the family was reunited, night had fallen, so she returned to the palace with nothing.

The King took the objects from the first two Princesses, and then turned to the third. "What did you bring?" he asked.

"I'm afraid I don't have anything," the Princess explained apologetically. "I had to help a lost child find his mother."

The other two Princesses laughed with delight. How stupid the third Princess had been!

The King nodded his head thoughtfully. "Thank you for your objects," he said to the Princesses. "For tomorrow's task, I will hide an item in the palace that you must bring back to me."

"What will you hide?" the first Princess asked.

"I'm not going to tell you," the King said, "but if you are my daughter, you will know it is something very special to us."

The next day, the Princesses searched the palace for the hidden item.

The first Princess returned with a luxurious string of pearls that belonged to the Queen.

The second Princess handed over an intricately carved silver goblet.

The third Princess hunted high and low until eventually she found a small thimble hidden under a pillow in one of the bedrooms. The other Princesses snickered when they saw what she'd chosen to bring. The thimble was worthless!

"Why did you bring this?" the King asked.

The Princess smiled. "When I was a little girl, we used to enjoy playing hunt-the-thimble around the palace. This thimble brings back many special memories for our family."

"I see," the King said. "Now for your final, and hardest, task. You must bring us the most precious gift on Earth."

All of the Princesses thought hard about what their precious gift should be.

The first Princess decided on a bag of golden coins, which she piled high in front of the King's throne.

The second Princess chose a chest filled with rubies and sapphires, which she presented to the Queen.

They were both certain that the King and Queen would choose one of them as the Princess. They knew they had performed well in their tasks, much better

than the third Princess, who had very little to show for herself.

The third Princess stood in front of the King and Queen, but wasn't carrying anything.

"This is now the second task where you have returned empty-handed," the King said to the third Princess.

"I am not empty-handed," the Princess replied. "You asked us to bring you the most precious gift on Earth. You are my parents, and I have brought my love for you."

The King and Queen looked at each other and smiled. There was no doubt in their minds who their daughter was.

The Queen spoke. "Girls, although you have brought us precious objects and worldly riches, only one of you has demonstrated the kindness, generosity, and thoughtfulness of a true Princess." The Queen held out her arms to the third Princess and smiled. "Daughter, we know it's you. You've behaved graciously, as we've always taught you to do. Well done."

As the Queen spoke the words, the sorcerer's spell was broken, and the two fake Princesses disappeared in a puff of smoke. The Princess ran to her parents, who hugged her.

The next day, the Princess attended the party to celebrate her birthday. After the crown was placed on the Princess's head, the King, Queen, and all the people in the kingdom sang and danced at the most joyful celebration the kingdom had ever known.

The Princess and the Frog

Princess Thea was bored. She lived in a beautiful castle full of more toys than any girl could wish for, but she didn't feel like playing with any of them.

"What can I do?" she asked her father, the King.

"You could read a book," he suggested, brightly. Thea shook her head. "Draw a picture? Sew a lovely tapestry especially for me?"

Thea didn't want to do any of those things. With a big, fed-up sigh, she picked up her gold ball and wandered down to the lake at the far end of the castle gardens. It was a glorious summer day and her ball glistened in the sunlight as she tossed it up and caught it again. Wondering if she could make it reach the very top of the tallest tree in the garden, she threw the ball up as high as she could.

"Yes!" she cheered to herself, as it brushed the tip of the topmost branch. On its way down, though, it bounced off another branch and landed right in the middle of the lake.

"Oh, no!" cried Thea. "My ball! I can't reach it there!" She found a branch to try and get her ball back, but it was nowhere near long enough. She tried throwing stones at the ball to make it float toward the edge of the lake, but they only skidded off and seemed to push it farther away. There was nothing else to do but sit down and burst into tears.

"Please don't cry, Princess," said a voice from the grass nearby. Thea looked around eagerly, hoping to see someone who could help, but all she spotted was a little frog.

"You didn't say that…did you?" she asked.

"Of course I did," chuckled the frog. "Do you see anyone else around here?"

23

"No," Thea replied, "but frogs don't normally talk."
"They don't–normally," agreed the frog, winking
one of his goggle eyes. "But I'm special, and if you
promise to let me come and stay at the castle with
you tonight, I'll get your ball for you."
"Stay at the castle?" echoed the Princess.
"That's right," nodded the frog. "Eat your food,
sleep in your bed, that sort of thing."
Princess Thea gazed at him. She didn't really
want a frog croaking all the way through
dinner or leaving slime on her silk pillows.
"I'll give you some gold coins instead,"
she offered.
"What would I do with gold coins?"
scoffed the frog.
"I don't know," shrugged Thea. "I thought perhaps you might like shiny things."
"I think you're confusing me with a magpie," said the frog, "or maybe it's a crow.
I can never remember which. As you can see, I'm neither…and besides, you're
the one crying over a gold ball."
Thea looked at her dear ball, stranded in the lake. She'd treasured it since she
was little and really did want it back.
"All right," she agreed. "It's a deal."
The frog scrambled down the bank and hopped from lily pad to lily pad until
he reached the middle of the lake. Diving into the murky green water, he swam
behind the ball and pushed it along with his nose toward the water's edge until
the Princess could reach it. To his disappointment, she snatched up the ball and
ran back toward the castle with it, leaving him behind.
"Wait! What about your promise?" the frog called after her. "Don't I even get a
'thank you'?"

A few moments after Princess Thea had sat down at the table for dinner with her father that evening, there was a knock at the door.

"Princess, there is some…one to see you," announced the puzzled head butler.

He stood aside, being careful not to tread on the frog at his feet.

"Oh, um, hello," mumbled the Princess, feeling a little annoyed that the frog had followed her.

"Hello, Princess," said the frog. "You dashed off without me."

"A talking frog!" exclaimed the King. "How splendid! I don't recall meeting one before. Are you a friend of Thea's?"

"Yes," replied the frog. "She said I could come and stay for dinner and a sleepover if I got her ball from the lake, but then she ran away."

"Is this true?" the King asked his daughter.

"Well, yes," she admitted. "I wanted my ball back. He's just a frog…"

"It's very important to keep your promises," said the King, firmly. "I've told you that before."

He turned to the frog and summoned him to the table with a wave of his hand. Princess Thea tried not to grimace as the frog made himself comfortable on the table by her plate and a meal was brought for him. She was surprised to see him eat almost as much as she did.

"You have a big appetite for a small frog," she sniffed.

The frog followed the Princess around for the rest of the evening, sharing her toys and joining in her games. She only agreed to play with him to make the time pass more quickly, so that the moment for him to leave might come sooner.

At last, it was bedtime. The Princess said goodnight to her father and went up the huge staircase to her room, with the frog hopping along behind her. She got ready for bed and was snuggling down into her covers when she felt the frog padding around on her pillow, trampling on her hair.

"What do you think you're doing?" she asked, sitting up and wiping her hair in disgust. "I'll get you a cushion to sleep on."

Thea got up and grabbed a cushion from her reading chair.

"Here," she said to the frog, putting the cushion on the floor. "You can sleep on this. It's far more comfortable than any of the lily pads you're used to."

The frog refused to move; the Princess had said she would let him share her bed and a promise was a promise.

"I'll never get to sleep with a frog right next to my head!" wailed the Princess, tears filling her eyes.

"All right," the frog said gently, not wanting to see her upset. "If you would like me to go now, there's just one thing you need to do."

"What's that?" Thea asked hopefully.

"Kiss me," the frog replied.

"Kiss you?" gasped Thea.

She was about to cry again, until she realized that a kiss would be over in a second; then she would be free of the horrible frog. She knelt next to her bed and leaned on her elbows toward him. The frog shut his eyes as her lips touched his in a gentle kiss. The Princess gasped as a burst of sparkling dust immediately

27

exploded from him and she jumped back in alarm as he turned into the most handsome boy she had ever seen.

"Thank you," he grinned, returning the Princess's kiss. "You just broke the spell!"

"What spell?" asked Thea, astonished.

"A witch disguised as a beggar woman turned me into a frog when I wouldn't buy a lucky charm from her," the boy explained. "She said the spell would only be broken when I spent the night with a Princess who would kiss me. Now I'm a Prince again!"

"A Prince!" exclaimed the Princess, blushing. "And to think I ran away from you when you helped me!"

"Without even thanking me," the Prince teased. "Don't worry, I forgive you."

The Prince and Princess talked all night long. The next morning, they agreed that they would like to be married and announced their happy news over breakfast. The King was delighted that his daughter had fallen in love with a Prince.

"You see," he smiled to Thea, "keeping your promise was the right thing to do."

"Now I must go back to my own castle and tell my family that Princess Thea has saved me," said the Prince. "They've been so upset—they were sure that I was going to be a frog forever."

28

The Prince's mother and father were delighted to see that he was back to his handsome self. He introduced them to Princess Thea and she was immediately welcomed into the family.

Once they were old enough, the Prince and Princess were married in a huge wedding celebration by the lake where they had first met. They even had a beautiful five-tier cake with an unusual decoration at the top: a golden ball!

The Very Kind Princess

Once upon a time, there lived a Princess who was blessed with great beauty and a very kind heart.

One day, when it was raining and the Princess was bored, she decided to explore parts of the castle that she visited only once in a while. She lit a candle and went down the stone staircase into the cellar. Among the broken chairs and worn carpets, she spotted something glinting in the candlelight. The Princess climbed over some dusty picture frames and picked up an old lamp. She used the hem of her dress to give it a polish. To her astonishment, a genie appeared. The Princess was so shocked, she almost fainted.

"I have been imprisoned in this lamp for many years," said the genie. "Now you have released me and I have the power to grant you three wishes. But if I grant your wishes, I will have to return to the lamp. On the other hand, if you agree to do three things for me instead, I will be freed from the lamp forever."

The Princess was tempted to wish for a unicorn, which she'd always wanted, but she decided to help the genie because she always put other people's needs before her own.

"What can I do for you?" the Princess asked the genie.

"I would like you to bring me the flower of the magical mandragon plant," he said. "It can only be found in the Enchanted Forest, where it grows in the shade of the tallest tree, and that is all I want."

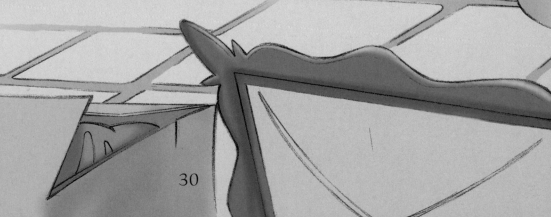

The Enchanted Forest was dark and frightening, and the Princess had heard that bears lived there but, nevertheless, she agreed, and set off to find the magical flower. The ground was wet underfoot and, before long, the Princess's shoes were soaked and the bottom of her dress was covered in mud.

"Oh dear, this task is a lot harder than I expected," the Princess said to herself, as she struggled through the tangled branches to the heart of the forest where the tallest tree stood. At last, she came upon the flower but, as she bent down to pick it, she heard something moving nearby. At first, she was worried that it might be a bear, but then she spotted a little curled horn poking through the leaves. Grasping the flower in one hand, the Princess peered into the bushes. Nestled in the undergrowth was a baby unicorn. The Princess was thrilled. It was all alone, so she helped it to its feet and gently led it out of the forest, so she could care for it back at the castle.

"I won't give this to the genie," she said to herself, "because he said that the flower was all he wanted."

When the Princess had settled her unicorn into one of the stables, she returned to the cellar. The genie was nowhere to be seen, so she picked up the lamp and rubbed it once more with the hem of her dress. The genie appeared instantly and she gave him the magical flower.

"Thank you for fulfilling my first request," he said. "Now, I only need you to complete two more tasks for me and I will be freed from the lamp forever."

The Princess also longed to wish for a beautiful necklace, but she was a kind and generous girl and wanted to help the genie.

"What can I do for you?" she asked.

"I would like you to bring me a precious pure white pearl," he said. "It can only be found at the bottom of the Mystical Lake, and that is all I want."

 The Princess hated swimming, and it was said that a giant serpent lived in the Mystical Lake, but she wanted to help the genie, so she made her way to the lake, took a deep breath and jumped into the cold, deep water. She swam down to the bottom and searched through the mud until she found a pure white pearl. She was about to swim back up when she spotted something red and shiny. At first, she was worried that it might be the eye of a serpent, but then she saw a golden clasp.

It was the most beautiful ruby necklace, which looked as if it had been lost for years. She scooped it up and reached the surface just before she ran out of breath. Gasping for air, she climbed out of the freezing water and hurried back to the castle, where she laid the beautiful ruby necklace on a velvet cushion in her bedroom.

"I won't give this to the genie," she said to herself, "because he said that the pearl was all he wanted."

As before, there was no sign of the genie in the cellar when she went back, so she rubbed the lamp again, and he reappeared.

"Thank you fulfilling my second request," he said, as she gave him the pure white pearl. "Now, I have one final thing to ask of you."

The Princess would have liked to have used the last wish for herself and wished for a handsome Prince to take her to the ball that evening, but she wanted the genie to be free.

"What can I do for you?" she asked.

"My last request is simple," the genie said. "All I ask for is a pink rose."

The Princess thought this would be easy and she hurried straight to the royal rose garden. But when she got there, she looked at the garden in dismay.

It was badly overgrown and every rose she could see was red. At last, she spotted a single pink flower, but it was right in the middle of the garden. As the Princess fought her way through the bushes, the thorns ripped her dress. She tried hard not to cry—she was cold and wet, her shoes were ruined, and now her dress was not just covered in mud, it was torn, as well.

Yet, the Princess was determined to complete her final task, so she struggled through the bushes, picked the pink rose, and returned with it to the cellar. She rubbed the lamp and the genie appeared.

"Thank you for fulfilling my third request," he said. "You have freed me forever!" At that moment, the Princess was dazzled by a magical, sparkling light that encircled the genie and lit up the cellar's darkest corners. When she could see clearly again, the genie had disappeared and, in his place, stood a tall and handsome Prince.

"I was once cold-hearted and thought only of myself," the Prince explained. "To punish me for my selfish ways, a witch put a spell on me, trapping me in that lamp until I could find someone who was willing to complete three tasks for me out of the goodness of their heart. Now I would like to use the last of my magic to do something for you."

There was another flash of blinding light and, in an instant, the Princess's muddy, wet, and torn dress was replaced by a beautiful ball gown. The Prince took her hand and asked if she would accompany him to the ball that evening.

All the Princess's wishes had been granted and, in time, the Prince and Princess were married. The unicorn was a guest at their wedding, and the bride carried a bouquet of pink roses arranged around a magical mandragon flower. On her finger was a pure white pearl ring and she wore a beautiful ruby necklace.

Snow White

Long, long ago, in midwinter, a beautiful Queen sat sewing at her window, which had a frame of black ebony wood. As she sewed, she pricked her finger and three drops of blood fell onto the snow on her windowsill. The red blood on the white snow against the black wood looked so beautiful that she thought, "If only I had a child with skin as white as snow, lips as red as blood, and hair as black as ebony." Soon, she had a little daughter with snow-white skin, blood-red lips, and ebony-black hair. She was named Princess Snow White, but sadly, shortly after her birth, the Queen died.

A year passed and the King married again. His new wife was beautiful, but very vain. She owned a magic mirror and, each morning, she would ask, "Mirror, mirror on the wall, who is the fairest one of all?"

And every day the mirror would answer, "You are the fairest one of all."
However, as Snow White grew older, she became more and more beautiful.
One day, the Queen asked, "Mirror, mirror on the wall, who is the fairest
one of all?"
The mirror, which always spoke the truth, replied, "O Lady Queen, though fair
you be, Snow White is fairer far to see."
The Queen grew so jealous of Snow White that she ordered a huntsman to
take the Princess into the woods and kill her. As proof that she was dead, the
huntsman was to return with her heart. The huntsman could not disobey the
Queen, so he took Snow White into the woods, but when the time came to
kill her, he took pity on the girl and told her to run away and hide instead.
He returned to the palace with the heart of a deer and told the Queen that it
belonged to Snow White.

Meanwhile, alone in the dark forest, Snow White stumbled over sharp stones and through thorn bushes until, just as the sun was about to set, she came across a little house. She went inside and found that everything was very small. There was a little table with seven little plates, seven little spoons, seven little knives and forks, and seven little mugs. Against the wall were seven little beds.

Snow White was so hungry and thirsty that she took a little of the food from each plate and drank a few drops from each mug. Then, because she was so tired, she tried each of the little beds, but none felt right until she came to the seventh one, so she lay down on it and fell asleep.

As night fell, the seven dwarfs who lived in the little house came home. They lit their seven little candles, and saw that someone had been in their house.

"Who has been sitting on my chair?" asked the first.

"Who has been eating from my plate?" asked the second.

"Who has taken a piece of my bread?" asked the third.

"Who has been eating my vegetables?" asked the fourth.

"Who has been using my fork?" asked the fifth.

"Who has been cutting with my knife?" asked the sixth.

"Who has been drinking out of my mug?" asked the seventh.

Then they noticed that the beds were rumpled and the seventh dwarf found Snow White asleep in his. She looked so beautiful and peaceful, they decided to let her sleep until morning.

When Snow White woke up, the dwarfs crowded around her asking why she was in their house. Snow White told them her story and they took pity on the girl.

"If you will keep our house tidy, you can stay here," they said. "We spend the days digging for gold in the mine and you can have our supper ready when we come home. But the wicked Queen may come looking for you, so don't let anyone in."

That morning, the Queen asked her mirror, "Mirror, mirror on the wall, who is the fairest one of all?"

The mirror replied, "O Lady Queen, though fair you be, Snow White is fairer far to see."

"Over the hills and far away, she lives with seven dwarfs today."

When the Queen found out that the huntsman had deceived her, she flew into a rage. She knew that the seven dwarfs lived in the seven mountains, so she disguised herself as an old peddler woman and made her way to their house.

The Queen knocked at the door and Snow White peered through the window. Seeing that it was only an old woman, she opened the door.

"I have silk laces of every shade," said the Queen. "Let me try this pretty one on your dress."

The Queen threaded the lace through Snow White's dress and tied it so tightly, that the Princess fell down as if she were dead.

When the dwarfs came home, they found Snow White lying on the ground. But when they cut the silk lace, she drew a long breath and slowly came back to life. "That peddler woman was certainly the wicked Queen," they said. "Now, do not open the door to anyone in future."

The moment the Queen got home, she said to her mirror, "Mirror, mirror on the wall, who is the fairest one of all?"

Again the mirror answered, "O Lady Queen, though fair you be, Snow White is fairer far to see. Over the hills and far away, she lives with seven dwarfs today."

The Queen was furious, so she made a poisoned comb, disguised herself differently and went back to the little house. This time, when she knocked on the door, Snow White called out, "I am not allowed to let anyone in." However, when the girl looked out of the window and saw the beautiful comb, she opened the door.

"Let me comb your hair," offered the Queen. The moment she put the comb in Snow White's hair, the girl fell to the ground.

The dwarfs came home just in time and pulled the poisoned comb from Snow White's hair.

Back at the palace, the Queen went straight to her mirror.

"Mirror, mirror on the wall, who is the fairest one of all?" she asked.

Yet again the mirror answered, "O Lady Queen, though fair you be, Snow White is fairer far to see. Over the hills and far away, she lives with seven dwarfs today."

Trembling with anger, the wicked Queen went into her most secret room and made a poisoned apple. Then she disguised herself as a peasant woman and knocked on the door of the dwarfs' house.

Snow White peeped out and called, "I'm not allowed to let anyone in."

"I am selling these apples," said the peasant woman. "Here, I will give you one to taste."

The apples looked red and juicy so Snow White was very tempted to take a bite.

"I will cut the apple in two and eat half of it," said the Queen. Now, the apple had been cleverly made so that only half was poisoned.

When Snow White saw that the peasant woman was eating part of the apple, she took the other half through the window. She bit into it and fell down dead.

That evening the dwarfs returned home and found Snow White lying dead. There was nothing they could do to help her, so they had a glass coffin made and laid her inside. Snow White lay in the coffin, close to the dwarfs' house in the forest, for many years, but she remained as beautiful as ever. She looked as if she were just sleeping.

Now when the Queen asked, "Mirror, mirror on the wall, who is the fairest one of all?" She was pleased to hear the reply, "You are the fairest one of all."

One day a young Prince was riding through the forest and came across Snow White's coffin. He was enchanted by her beauty and begged the dwarfs to let him have it. As his servants lifted it up, the piece of poisoned apple fell from Snow White's throat, and she awakened. The Prince declared his love for her and their wedding was planned.

The next time the Queen asked her mirror, "Mirror, mirror on the wall, who is the fairest one of all?" the mirror answered, "You, my Queen, are fair, it is true. But the young Queen is a thousand times fairer than you."

Filled with jealousy, the Queen decided to go to the wedding. When she arrived and saw that the bride was Snow White, she ran toward the happy couple in a fury. She was seized by the palace guards and, as punishment for her wicked ways, she was banished from the kingdom for ever.

The Princess and the Rainbow

Once upon a time there was a Princess called Arabella, who lived in a faraway land with many fairies. Princess Arabella took special care of the fairies, because they had a very important job. Whenever the sun shone and it rained at the same time, the fairies used their magic to make beautiful rainbows. There was a fairy in charge of each of the shades that made up a rainbow—red, orange, yellow, green, blue, indigo, and violet.

The fairies loved their work and were very happy. They knew they had the best job in the world, because whenever anyone saw a rainbow, they were instantly filled with joy.

"Ahhhh," children chorused in awe, as the brightness filled the sky.

"Oooooh," women and men smiled in amazement, with huge grins on their faces.

"What a wonderful sight," people would comment, pausing to stop and stare at the rainbow arching above their heads.

Whenever they heard the praise for their creations, the fairies were delighted. They enjoyed nothing more than hearing everyone compliment their rainbows.

"Well done," the Princess said, whenever the fairies had returned from painting the bright stripes across the sky. "You're all so good at making everyone smile. Everyone admires what you do."

Princess Arabella loved her fairy family, but she always kept a close eye on them. The Princess knew that although the fairies were sweet and good-natured, they also had a mischievous side.

One day, the Princess was very tired, so she decided to lie down under a shady tree and take a nap. As soon as her eyes closed, Fairy Violet had an idea.

"The Princess is fast asleep," she whispered to her friends. "Things have been so boring around here lately. Let's have some fun!"

Fairy Red's eyes twinkled. "Let's change everything so it looks completely different," she said. "People love our rainbows. Let's put them everywhere!"

"Yes, let's," all the fairies chorused, giggling with glee. They flew off around the land in a blur of golden wings.

Fairy Blue waved her wand. All of the trees in the kingdom became orange and yellow striped.

Fairy Green cast a spell and made the grass indigo.

Fairy Yellow turned the sun violet using magical sparkles.

Soon everything in the kingdom looked completely different.

"Look at how pretty everything is now!" Fairy Violet said, contentedly.

When the Princess awoke, she heard the sound of delighted giggling. She sat up and yawned, then blinked in astonishment. Everything around her had been transformed into rainbow shades.

"What's happened?" Princess Arabella wondered. Then suddenly she understood. "Oh, no! It must have been the fairies. I hope they can change everything back again quickly. I don't have a good feeling about this."

The Princess called the fairies to her. "You've been causing mischief while I've been sleeping, haven't you?" she said.

The fairies all laughed and scampered around in the violet sunshine. They were thrilled with their trick.

"I'd like you turn things back to the way they're supposed to be," the Princess said, then she held out her hand and gasped. "But it will have to wait. It's started raining. Fairies, you need to make a rainbow!"

The fairies darted into the air and flew away at top speed. They busily painted a rainbow and soon, curved stripes were reaching across the sky. The fairies fluttered back down to earth and admired their creation.

"Look," Fairy Orange said, nudging Fairy Red. "Some people are coming. Watch their faces when they see what we've done."

But the fairies were astonished when no 'ooohs' or 'aaahs' of pleasure came. Nobody said a word about how beautiful the rainbow was. In fact, everyone ignored it completely.

The fairies were dismayed. This had never happened before! What had gone wrong? They rushed away to find the Princess.

"You have to help us," Fairy Violet pleaded, tugging at Princess Arabella's sleeve. "No one liked the rainbow we made. Everybody just walked past and didn't make a sound. We're not making people happy anymore. Princess, what should we do?"

Princess Arabella looked up at the sky and immediately knew what the problem was. "It's because it's difficult to see," the Princess explained. "After your mischief-making, everything in the land is bright. You've mixed everything up so much that nobody can see the rainbow."

"Oh, no," the fairies gasped. Fairy Red started to cry.

The Princess felt sorry for the fairies. She knew the fairies hadn't meant to cause trouble. She gave Fairy Red a comforting hug.

"Dry your tears," she said. "All you have to do is magic everything back to how it was before. Then everyone will be able to see your pretty rainbows again and they'll be happy."

The fairies quickly did as they were told, sprinkling magic dust and waving their wands. They transformed everything in the land back to normal. Once they'd finished, the fairies sat in the sunshine and waited.

"There's a dark cloud coming," Fairy Blue said excitedly, pointing to the sky.

The fairies held out their hands and, before long, felt the pitter-patter of rainfall on their tiny palms.

"Let's go," Fairy Indigo said, leaping to her feet and darting into the air.

Quickly the other fairies joined her, painting an arch that spread across the sky.

It was the biggest and prettiest rainbow they'd ever made, and by the time they'd finished, they were all tired.

There was a gasp from below. "Look at that wonderful rainbow," a mother said to her daughter.

"Ooooh," the little girl said. "I'm going to draw one just like it when I get home." Quickly a large crowd gathered, all gazing upward with wide smiles on their faces.

The fairies flew back to the Princess. "Everyone loves our rainbows again," Fairy Yellow said with relief.

"I'm glad," the Princess said.

From that day, the fairies didn't make any more mischief. They have made a lot more rainbows though, and they know everyone always enjoys them.

Sleeping Beauty

Once upon a time, there lived a King and Queen, who longed for a child. After many years, the Queen at last gave birth to a daughter. The King and Queen were delighted and invited everyone in the kingdom to attend the christening at the castle chapel. They chose seven fairies to be godmothers to the new Princess and, at the ceremony, each bestowed a gift upon the baby. The first wished that the Princess should grow up to be the most beautiful girl in the world; the second, that she should have the wit of an angel; the third, that she should have grace in everything she did; the fourth, that she should dance perfectly; the fifth, that she should sing like a nightingale; and the sixth, that she should play all kinds of music to perfection.

The seventh fairy, however, was something of a witch and she was angry because she was the last to have been invited to the christening. She, too, had something for the baby, but it was a curse, not a blessing–the old fairy wished that the Princess should have her hand pierced by a spindle and die of the wound. One of the other fairies overheard the wicked curse and, although she was unable to undo it, she cast a spell so that, instead of dying, the Princess would fall into a deep sleep, which would last for one hundred years, after which time she would be awoken by the kiss of a King's son.

The King immediately ordered that every spindle in the kingdom be burned, so that the evil fairy's curse could not be fulfilled. As the years went by, the young Princess grew into the most beautiful girl in the whole kingdom and filled her parents' lives with joy. One day, when she was 16-years-old and her parents were away, the Princess was bored and decided to explore the castle. She came across a door she had never noticed before. She opened it and discovered a spiral staircase that led up to a high tower. When she reached the little room right at the top, she found an old woman spinning with a spindle. Having never seen such a thing before, the Princess asked if she could try spinning herself. The old woman agreed, but as soon as the girl touched the spindle, it pierced her hand and she fell to the ground. The old woman, who had not heard that all spindles should be destroyed and meant the Princess no harm, summoned help immediately, but no one could revive her.

When the King and Queen heard the news, they ordered that the Princess should be laid upon a bed embroidered with gold and silver in one of the finest apartments in the castle. Although her eyes were shut, the Princess continued to breathe softly and she remained as beautiful as an angel. The King commanded that she should not be disturbed, but left to sleep quietly till the hour of her awakening.

The good fairy, who had saved the life of the Princess by condemning her to sleep for 100 years, was far away when the accident happened, but, as soon as she heard the news, she hurried to the palace in a fiery chariot drawn by dragons.

The good fairy did not want the Princess to find herself all alone when she woke up so she cast a spell on everyone in the palace, including the King and Queen. Governesses, ladies-in-waiting, cooks, scullery maids, guards, pages, and footmen, as well as all the dogs and horses, fell asleep as soon as she touched them with her wand, ready to awake with the Princess and serve her when she needed them.

Within less than an hour, a huge number of trees, bushes, and brambles had grown up and entwined themselves around the castle, so that neither man nor beast could pass through. All that could be seen of it were the very tops of the towers.

One hundred years later, the son of a King from a distant realm was on a hunting trip and noticed the towers that were almost hidden from view within a great thick wood.

He asked the local people what they were. Some told him that it was a ruined castle, haunted by spirits. Others, that it was a meeting place for all the sorcerers and witches in the country. However, the common opinion was that it was home to an ogre, who was the only person to have the power to pass through the wood. The Prince didn't know what to believe. Then a good countryman told him, "May it please your Royal Highness, my father heard my grandfather say that in this castle lies the most beautiful Princess ever seen. She is under a spell and must sleep there for one hundred years until she is awakened by a King's son."

The young Prince was very excited to hear this and decided to try to reach the castle himself. As he fought his way through the tangled wood, the great trees, bushes, and brambles suddenly gave way to let him through, but after he passed by, they immediately closed again so no one was able to follow him. The Prince walked through the castle gates and into a spacious courtyard, where there were stretched-out bodies of men and animals, all appearing to be fast asleep.

He climbed the stairs and came to the guard chamber, where guards were standing with their muskets upon their shoulders, snoring as loudly as they could. After that, he passed through rooms full of ladies and gentlemen, all fast asleep, some standing, others sitting. At last he came to a gilded chamber and saw a gold and silver bed, upon which lay a most beautiful Princess. He approached with trembling and admiration, and fell down before her on his knees. Then he kissed her lovely ruby lips.

He had broken the spell and the Princess woke up and gazed at the handsome young man. "Is it you, my Prince?" she asked. "You have waited a long time." The Prince was charmed by these words and assured her that he loved her better than he did himself. They talked together for hours, and yet they still had far more to say.

In the meantime, everyone else in the palace woke up and went back about their business—cooking, cleaning, and tending to the animals. The chief lady-in-waiting grew very impatient and told the Princess that supper was being served. The Prince helped the Princess to rise from her bed and she was soon reunited with her mother and father.

As quickly as they had grown up, the tangled trees, bushes, and brambles encircling the palace died back and disappeared. The following day, the Prince asked the Princess to be his wife. They were married in the castle chapel and lived happily ever after.

The Enchanted Forest

Once upon a time, there was a Princess who lived in a grand palace with her father, the King, her stepmother, the Queen, and her two stepsisters. Although the Princess was always surrounded by servants, she was very lonely. She tried to make friends with her stepsisters, but they weren't always kind and never wanted to play with her. There weren't any other boys or girls in the palace, so there wasn't anyone else for the Princess to play with. The Princess spent a lot of time alone.

"I wish I had a best friend," thought the Princess sadly, as she walked through the palace gardens. She stopped to admire the beautiful roses, which grew beside the perfect lawns. The Princess wished she had someone to pick the pretty flowers for and to run with across the grass.

One day, the Princess heard her stepsisters laughing in the Queen's bedroom. They were dressing up in the Queen's finest clothes and trying on all her best jewels. The two sisters were smiling and joking as they twirled across the floor wearing splendid ball gowns.

"Please can I play dress up, too?" asked the Princess, eagerly.

Her stepsisters looked at her scornfully. "You're not big enough," the eldest sister said. "These clothes won't fit you," added her younger sister. "Why don't you go play outside?"

62

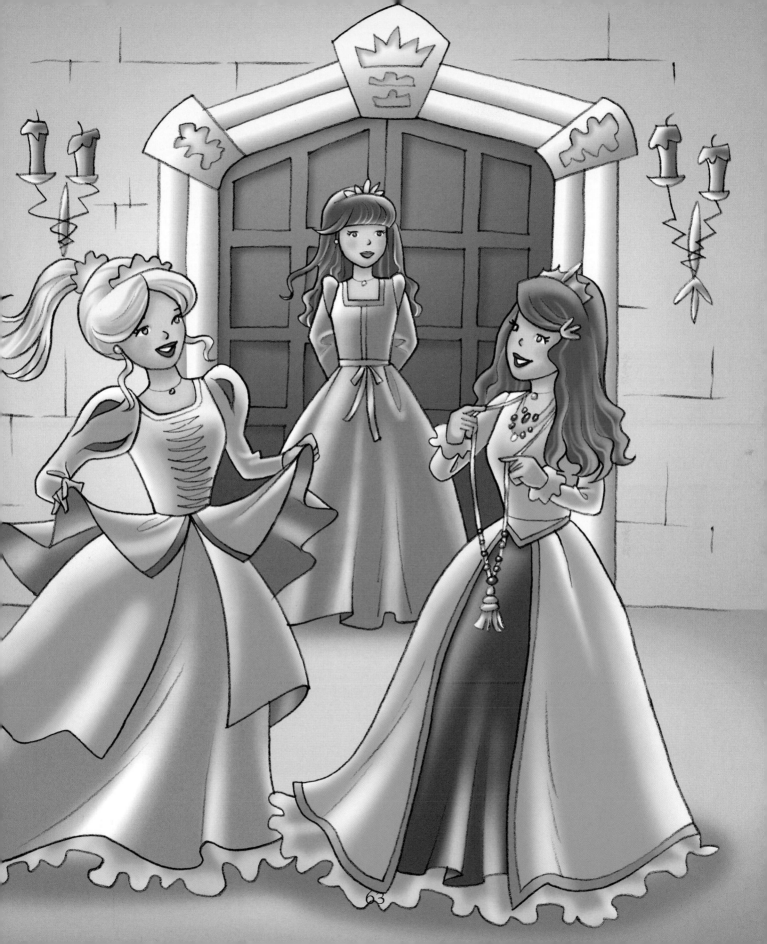

"But I'd really like to stay here, with you," the Princess pleaded. She couldn't bear to spend another day on her own.

"You can't," said the younger sister, putting on a sparkling tiara and admiring her reflection in the mirror.

"Go away and leave us alone," said the older sister, turning her back on the Princess.

The Princess went downstairs and into the gardens. A tear ran down her cheek as she started to explore the path that led into the woods. The leaves on the trees rustled and whispered invitingly as she wandered further and further into the forest.

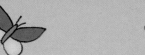 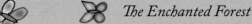

The Princess walked until she saw a clearing ahead, where sunlight was streaming through the trees. She ran toward it and gasped in amazement. Standing in front of her was a beautiful unicorn! The unicorn pawed at the ground with a graceful leg as the sun's rays glistened on its golden horn. It stared at the Princess and she hesitated. She knew unicorns were very shy and she didn't want to startle it. "Hello," said the Princess softly. "You're the most beautiful creature I've ever seen."

The unicorn tossed its head and trotted over. It lowered its nose and allowed the Princess to gently stroke its silky coat.

"Unicorn, will you be my friend?" the Princess asked. The unicorn nuzzled its head into the Princess's arm.

The Princess was happier than she'd ever been. She sat down on the ground next to the unicorn and told it how lonely she was, how her stepsisters wouldn't let her play with them, and how she longed for a friend. Although the unicorn didn't speak, the Princess could tell it was listening carefully.

When the Princess had finished talking, the unicorn trotted over to the side of the clearing and looked back at the Princess.

"Do you want me to follow you?" the Princess asked.

The unicorn nodded, and the Princess followed it through the forest. Soon, the trees thinned and there was silver grass beneath their feet. The Princess gazed around. She was surrounded by vibrant red, purple, and turquoise trees, and a rainbow stream flowed nearby. There were beautiful flowers and the sky was baby pink with fluffy blue clouds drifting across it. The Princess couldn't believe her eyes. It was all so unusual, and was totally different to anything she'd ever seen before. The unicorn had led her into an enchanted land!

"Where are we?" the Princess asked. The unicorn stopped walking and stamped its foot three times. Before she knew what was happening, the Princess was surrounded by friendly faces. She gasped as she saw fairies fluttering around her.

"Hello," one of the fairies said, in a voice that sounded like musical notes. "Who are you?"

"I'm a Princess from the kingdom on the other side of the forest," the Princess replied.

"A Princess," the fairies gasped with glee, clapping their hands together. They flew around excitedly. "We've never met a real Princess before."

"I've never met a real fairy before, either," the Princess said shyly. "Or a unicorn, for that matter."

"Stay with us for a while," one of the fairies begged. "We'd love to play with you. We hope you'll be our friend."

"You'd like to be my friend?" the Princess asked.

"Of course!" the fairies replied.

The Princess had a wonderful time. The fairies showed the Princess around the enchanted land. Then she played hide-and-seek with them, which the fairies won easily, because it's very difficult to find a fairy when she's hiding. After that, the Princess ate delicious tiny buttercup muffins and wild cherry tarts. She'd never had so much fun.

At the end of the afternoon, the purple sun began to set in the green sky.

"I'd better go," the Princess said, sadly.

"You'll come back though, won't you?" one of the fairies asked. "We've had such a lovely time with you."

"Of course I will," the Princess replied, smiling happily. "I'm lucky to have made so many wonderful new friends. I'll see you tomorrow!"

The fairies waved good-bye as the Princess walked back through the trees. When she got home, her stepsisters were waiting, and they said they were sorry for not letting her join in. The girls became good friends and the Princess introduced them to the fairies in the enchanted land. They all played happily together and, from that day on, the Princess was never lonely again.

The Princess and the Pea

Once upon a time there was a handsome Prince, who was heir to a very wealthy kingdom. When he came of age, his mother, the Queen, decided that it was time for him to find a bride. But before the Prince set off on his quest to find a future wife, she gave him some important advice. He should look for a girl who was beautiful, but also well-born, with elegance and good manners. Above all, he should make sure that his bride-to-be was a real Princess. True Princesses, said his mother, were very delicate and sensitive. The Prince journeyed far and wide and was introduced to many ladies of noble birth. However, the young man was not easy to please and, although he met many pretty girls, not one of them was quite right.

As he was walking in the garden with the first girl, a butterfly landed on her shoulder. She looked shocked, as if she'd just been hit by a heavy branch. Clearly, she was very sensitive, so she must be a true Princess. But over lunch, the Prince noticed that she spoke with her mouth full and was rude to the servants. He knew that his parents wouldn't approve of such bad manners, so he left and continued his search.

The next girl he met was beautiful and sweet-natured, but when he accidentally stepped on her toe, she hardly seemed to notice. Although she seemed perfect in every way, she obviously wasn't very delicate and sensitive, so she couldn't possibly be a real Princess. Reluctantly, he said good-bye to her and went on his way.

Each time the young man met a young lady he remembered his mother's words and, sadly, not a single one of the girls matched up to all her demands. They were either beautiful but ill-mannered, charming but not very attractive, or had good looks and good manners but were not delicate or sensitive enough to be real Princesses.

Eventually, the Prince had no choice but to return to the palace and tell his disappointed parents that none of the girls he had met were suitable.

One evening, the kingdom was hit by a terrible storm. Lightning flashed around the towers of the palace and the thunder was so loud it felt as if the walls were shaking. A fierce wind rattled the doors and windows, all the dogs started to howl and rain fell from the sky in torrents, hammering on the roof. Amid all this noise, the old King, the Prince's father, heard a loud banging on the door. He hurried to open it.

A flash of lightning revealed a young lady standing outside in the pouring rain. She was soaked through to the bone, her clothes were covered in mud, and dripping strands of hair clung to her face. She claimed to be a Princess and told the King that her carriage had slipped off the muddy road into a ditch. She had seen the palace in the distance and hoped they would give her shelter for the night.

The King invited her in and the Queen offered to lend the poor, ragged girl a change of clothes. As the Princess warmed up and dried her long, golden hair in front of the fire, the Prince realized that she was actually very beautiful. Then, as she ate her supper, he noticed that she had very good table manners. The pair chatted all evening and he discovered that she was very charming, too. He thought that he may finally have found his bride-to-be. His mother was suspicious, though, and decided to put the girl to the test to find out whether

she really was a true Princess.

The Queen asked the servants to lift up the mattress on the bed in the guest room, high up in one of the towers, and she placed a pea underneath it. Then she asked them to bring every spare mattress in the palace up to the room. There was much huffing and puffing as the servants carried mattresses up and down staircases, squeezed them through narrow doorways, and struggled to get them round tight corners. Eventually another 19 mattresses were crammed into the room and there was hardly space to move. The Queen instructed the puzzled servants to place all the mattresses on the bed, one on top of the other. Soon the pile of mattresses was too high for them to add any more and they had to fetch a ladder so they could carry on stacking them up. Luckily the room in the tower had a very high ceiling.

When, at last, the Princess was escorted to her room, she was rather surprised to see the huge pile of mattresses with a tall ladder leaning against them so she could climb into bed. However, she had come from a faraway kingdom and she thought this must be a strange local custom—and being a well-bred young lady, she was far too polite to mention the unusual bed.

The Princess was very tired after her long walk in the rain and she expected to fall asleep as soon as her head touched the pillow, but, in spite of the fact that she was lying on top of so many soft feather mattresses, she just couldn't get comfortable.

At first she thought she must be lying on the button of her nightgown, so she turned over, but she could still feel something in the bed.

Then she decided there must be a little clump of feathers in the top mattress, but she checked and it felt perfectly smooth.

The poor Princess tossed and turned all night and didn't get a wink of sleep. The next morning, the Queen asked her guest if the bed had been comfortable and whether she had slept well. The Princess didn't know what to say. She was a very considerate young lady, so she didn't want to be rude and complain about the bed, especially since the King and Queen had been kind enough to take her

in for the night. On the other hand she had been brought up to never tell a lie, so she couldn't say that she had had a good night's sleep either.

"Well," she said, hesitating, "the mattresses were lovely and soft–so soft, in fact, that I could feel a lump in the bed and when I checked in the morning I found a pea right at the bottom. I can't imagine how it got there, but I'm afraid it kept me awake all night and now I'm black and blue all over."

The Queen apologized to her guest, but secretly she smiled to herself. She had noticed that the Prince seemed very interested in the girl the previous evening and was pleased that now she could reassure him that this beautiful girl was, indeed, a true Princess.

"We've found a real Princess at last," she told her son, excitedly. "She is so sensitive, she felt the pea through 20 mattresses. Only a lady of gentle birth could do that."

The Prince was delighted. He had finally found the girl of his dreams and he asked her to marry him that very morning. He explained about the pea and all the mattresses and, luckily, the Princess thought it was very funny and burst out laughing. The pea was displayed at the happy couple's wedding, then it was placed it a gold and crystal box. It went on display at the palace museum, where it remains to this day.

The Princess's Great Surprise

Once upon a time, there was a King and Queen who lived in a beautiful kingdom. More than anything, they wanted a child and, before long, the Queen gave birth to a perfect baby girl named Rose. Everyone rejoiced at her arrival. The palace rang out with joyful cheering and there were feasts throughout the land to celebrate the wonderful news.

As time went on, the baby grew into a beautiful girl with long blond hair, big blue eyes, and a pink, rosebud mouth. The Princess had everything she could desire. She played with the best toys, ate the finest foods, and slept in the most magnificent bedroom in the palace. But there was something wrong. Princess Rose never smiled.

The King and Queen were extremely worried. "Daughter, what's wrong?" they asked over and over again. "Why aren't you happy?"

"I don't know," said Princess Rose. "There's no reason why I feel so sad. I just do."

"We have to get our wonderful girl to smile," the King said to his wife.

"I agree," said the Queen. "We must do everything we can to cheer her up."

The King and Queen thought hard about what might make their daughter laugh. Then the King came up with a brilliant idea. He would juggle for the Princess! He loved nothing more than watching court jugglers perform. The King borrowed some juggling balls and trained for a week until he was perfect.

"Watch this," the King said, sitting Princess Rose down on a throne.

The King threw the juggling balls above his head. He twisted and turned as the balls whizzed through the air. The King performed all the tricks he'd learned.

"Taaa-dddaaaaa!" the King said, swooping down into a bow.

The Princess clapped hard. She could see that her father had put a lot of effort into the act and she'd enjoyed it very much. But still she didn't smile.

"It's no good," the King said to the Queen. "The juggling didn't make her happy. Why don't you try something?"

It wasn't long before the Queen had an idea. She loved watching actors and actresses at the theater, so she decided to put on a play. The Queen called the finest playwright in the land and asked him to write the funniest play he could. Then she gathered actors and actresses together and instructed them to put on their best performances. The night of the show, the Queen was very excited.

As the curtain went up and the play began, the King and Queen roared with laughter. The performance was one of the funniest things they'd ever seen. But, although the Princess enjoyed herself, still she didn't laugh.

"I can't believe that didn't work," the Queen said. "The play was very amusing. But we mustn't give up. Something, somewhere, will make our beautiful daughter smile."

The King ordered his men to hang posters all over the kingdom.

The posters read:

"Wanted—the funniest jesters and clowns in all the land. Huge reward offered if you can make Princess Rose smile!"

Soon there was a long line outside the palace. Hundreds of people were convinced they would be the one to cheer up the Princess.

Princess Rose watched hundreds of acts. She saw clowns throwing custard pies, heard jesters telling jokes, and listened to musicians singing funny songs. The King and Queen laughed until their stomachs hurt but, still, the Princess didn't smile.

"Queen, what else can we do for our daughter?" the King asked in despair. "It breaks my heart to see her like this."

"I know," the Queen replied. "Maybe if these performers don't make her smile, a gift will. We must find the perfect present for her!"

The King and Queen contacted everyone they could think of, and another long line formed in front of the palace gates. People came from far and wide to present Princess Rose with riches far beyond her wildest dreams, but gold and silver couldn't make her happy. Rubies didn't work, emeralds were unsuccessful, and although the diamonds sparkled and twinkled, they still couldn't bring a smile to the Princess's face.

The King and Queen sank onto their thrones. The King dropped his head into his hands.

"I don't know what else to do," he murmured. "Our beautiful daughter is going to be sad forever and there's nothing we can do about it."

Just then, a small voice rang out across the empty hall. "Excuse me."

The King and Queen looked up to see a small boy standing in the doorway. He was holding a brightly patterned box.

"I've come to make Princess Rose smile," the little boy said.

The Queen shook her head. "It's no good," she said. "We've done everything. Absolutely everything. But our lovely girl just can't seem to laugh."

"I'd like to try something if I may, Your Majesty," the boy replied. "I've got something in this box that might just work."

The King and Queen eyed the object in the boy's hands. "What's in there?" asked the King curiously. "Is it a dragon's egg?"

"Or a fairy's wand?" the Queen added, eagerly.

"It's neither of those things," said the boy. "Please, may I see the Princess?"

"We've tried everything else," the King said wearily. "Let's give the child a chance."

The King and Queen led the boy through the corridors of the palace and soon they arrived at the Princess's bedroom. It was overflowing with all the incredible presents she'd been given. The Princess was sitting on her bed, looking unhappy. "Daughter, there's someone to see you," the Queen said. "He thinks he can make you smile."

When the boy held out the box, Princess Rose just stared at it sadly. The boy started to turn a handle on the side of the box and a happy, tinkling tune began to play. The Princess watched the box, her forehead still creased into a frown. The boy kept on turning the handle, faster and faster, until all of a sudden there was a loud POP! The top of the box flew open and a small painted doll burst out of it.

As the box popped open, Princess Rose jumped backward with a small shriek. Her eyes widened with surprise. . .and then it happened. The corners of her mouth twitched into a broad smile, and an unfamiliar noise filled the room. It started as a giggle, turned into a chuckle, then became a roar. The Princess was laughing at a Jack-in-the-Box!

Aladdin and Princess Suri

Princess Suri was reading beside one of the palace fountains when one of her servants came to see her.

"Your father is asking for you," said the servant. "A Prince has come to meet you."

Princess Suri sighed sadly. Suri was to marry before her next birthday, but she wished to marry for love, and Suri had not yet met a man that she could love.

"This Prince is very handsome," the servant told Suri, trying to cheer the Princess up.

"Handsome is no good if he is not kind, brave, and clever," Suri replied.

As she walked into her father's great hall, Suri saw a Prince dressed in the finest Arabian silks.

"My name is Prince Aladdin," he said.

Princess Suri looked at the Prince—he was indeed handsome.

"Can I spend the afternoon with you?" asked the Prince.

Suri sneaked a look at her book, she had just reached an exciting bit in the story and would much rather carry on reading than talk to this Prince. Prince Aladdin noticed this.

"You like stories?" he asked.

"Yes, very much," replied Suri.

"Then I will tell you a story of great adventure," offered the Prince.

Suri was pleased, and a little surprised—all the other Princes had only wanted to talk to her about how wealthy they were, or how handsome they were—so she agreed.

"My story is about a heroic young man," began the Prince. "Let us call him Aladdin."

"Like you?" asked Suri.

"It's as good a name as any," he replied, and continued with his story.

"Aladdin was the son of a tailor, who had died many years ago. He lived with his poor mother and looked after her as best he could. One day a stranger appeared claiming to be Aladdin's uncle. Aladdin's mother had never met her husband's brother, but the stranger was so kind and pleasant that they soon found it easy to believe he was Aladdin's uncle.

"However, the stranger was really an evil wizard, who had a wicked plan for which he needed the Aladdin's help.

"'Let us go for a walk around the city,' the wizard suggested one day.

"They walked through the market, then Aladdin's uncle took him to parts of the city he had never been to before. They stopped at the entrance to a cave.

"'Would you do something for me?' the wizard asked.

"Anything, Uncle," replied Aladdin.

"I need you to go into this cave," the wizard told him. "I am far too old to do it myself. Deep inside is hidden a treasure trove of jewels and gold, among the treasure you will find an old lamp. Bring it to me. You can keep the jewels for yourself, all I want is the lamp."

"The cave was dark and Aladdin was a little frightened, but he wanted to please his uncle, so he agreed.

"Aladdin walked through the long dark cave, for what felt like hours, until a huge mountain of gold stood before him, with rubies and emeralds, diamonds, and sapphires, all twinkling like Christmas lights.

"We will be rich now," he told himself. "Mother will not have to work anymore."

"Then Aladdin saw the lamp. It looked old and dirty next to the glittering treasure, but he picked it up, as it was what his uncle had asked for. As he began walking back, Aladdin felt the ground begin to shudder, and rocks began to tumble around him. Aladdin ran back up the tunnel as fast as he could to the entrance where his uncle waited.

"Throw the lamp out to me," the wizard instructed as Aladdin dodged the falling rocks.

"Aladdin found it strange that his uncle should be waiting a little way outside

the cave and not in the entrance.

"Give me your hand and help me out first," he suggested.

"Just give me the lamp!" cackled the wizard trying to snatch the lamp from Aladdin's hand. Aladdin jumped backward to stop the wizard getting the lamp just as a rockslide blocked the entrance to the cave, trapping Aladdin inside.

"The wizard quickly fled once his plan had failed, and without his lamp. Trapped in the cave, Aladdin grew very hungry, very weak, and very bored. He looked at the old lamp and decided to polish it so that it was as shiny as everything else in the glittering cave. Smoke began to pour out of the spout and a large man appeared in front of him.

"I am the genie of the lamp," he told Aladdin. 'You are my master and your wish is my command.'

"Can you get me out of here?" asked Aladdin.

"Certainly," replied the genie.

"There was a flash of light and then Aladdin was standing in the market square. Aladdin was so hungry that he ran to the nearest stall and started eating the fruit. But suddenly he was seized by two huge guards.

"Thief!" they shouted, "Lock him up!"

"Wait, I can pay for it," Aladdin tried to explain, but his clothes we so dirty from his time in the cave that the guards did not believe him.

"Stop," called a voice, the loveliest voice Aladdin had ever heard. He looked and saw a beautiful girl. "Can't you see that this poor man is hungry?" the girl asked. "He looks like he hasn't eaten in weeks. Let him go, I will pay for his food.'

"Of course, Princess Suri," said the guards, releasing Aladdin.

"Over the next few days Aladdin found himself thinking more and more about the lovely Princess. He used some of the jewels he had found to buy himself some nice clothes and decided to pay her a visit.

"And so here I am," said Aladdin, finishing his story.

91

Princess Suri clapped her hands in delight. She had thought it was such a wonderful story, but what she did not know was that it was all true.

Suri ran to tell her father that this was a Prince she could love and she would agree to the marriage, but when she arrived she found another man was already with the Sultan.

"This is my new adviser," he told her.

Aladdin saw at once that the adviser was the wizard who had pretended to be his uncle, and knew he would want to cause trouble.

"Sire," the wizard addressed the Sultan, "perhaps the Prince should give you a gift for your daughter?"

"But I don't need jewels," argued Suri.

Aladdin, however, agreed and gave the Sultan the some of the jewels he had found in the cave.

"Is this all your daughter is worth?" asked the wizard. "Have him return with forty of his servants, all bringing you jewels."

That night, Aladdin rubbed the lamp and the genie appeared again.

"Please send me forty servants each carrying jewels to the palace," asked Aladdin.

"Your wish is my command, Master," replied the genie.

Aladdin returned to the palace.

"Your servants arrived with the jewels," said the Sultan. "Now you may marry my daughter."

"Wait a minute, Sire," said the wizard. "Have you seen Aladdin's palace? Is it good enough for Suri?"

"Oh, it will be father," insisted Suri.

"Still, I should see it," replied the Sultan.

Once more, Aladdin called the genie.

"Please can you build me a palace as beautiful as the Princess?" Aladdin asked.

"Your wish is my command," the Genie replied.

Aladdin took Suri and the Sultan to see his new palace. The Sultan was amazed. It was built out of gorgeous white marble, with gold decoration on every wall. It was the most beautiful palace Suri had ever seen.

"I want my wedding to be held here," she cried with delight.

"Your wish is my command," replied Aladdin, smiling.

Their wedding was the grandest event anyone had ever seen. The Sultan's adviser vanished and was never heard from again. Aladdin kept the lamp safe and hidden, and was always thankful for the joy it had given him. He and Suri lived happily in their golden palace for the rest of their days.

Beauty and the Beast

Once upon a time there were three sisters who lived with their father in a small cottage on the edge of the woods.

The two older sisters were greedy and selfish, and thought of no one but themselves. But the youngest daughter, called Beauty, was pretty and kind. She loved her father very much. She knew he worked hard to look after the family, and she always did what she could to help him.

One day, their father had to go to the town on business.

"Be careful," said Beauty, as she handed him some food for the long journey.

Of course, the two older sisters were far too busy thinking about themselves to worry about him.

"Bring us back a present!" they cried greedily. "Be sure it is a big one!"

"What would you like?" asked their kindly father.

"A ruby ring!" replied the oldest.

"A silk dress!" cried her sister.

"What about you, my dear?" the father asked his youngest daughter.

Beauty thought for a moment. "All I desire is a red, red rose," she smiled.

Her father laughed. "I give you my word!" he said. "Be good girls while I am away. I shall be back by nightfall."

Their father kept his promise. When he had finished his business in the town, he went to buy presents for his daughters. First, he chose a sparkling ring and a beautiful silk dress for the two older girls. Then he searched for a rose for his gentle Beauty. But he couldn't find a flower seller anywhere.

"It's getting late," he decided. "I'm sure to find a rose to pick on my way home." So he climbed on his horse and set off.

On the way back, darkness fell quickly. Beauty's father looked about anxiously. There wasn't a single rose to be found anywhere. What was worse, he had been so busy searching, he hadn't noticed that he had taken a wrong turn. He was lost!

At last Beauty's father came to the gates of a great mansion.

"Maybe someone here can help me," he thought. He pushed open the gates and walked up the long driveway. He knocked at the front door–but there was no answer. He rang the bell–but there was still no answer. So he turned the doorknob and pushed. . .with a loud creak, the door swung open.

"Is anyone there?" he called, as he walked from room to room, searching for the owner. But though there was a roaring fire in the grate, and a delicious feast laid out on the table, no one was home.

The poor man was exhausted and very hungry and looked eagerly at the food.

"No one will mind if I just have a little," he convinced himself. He took a few small morsels of food and sat in a chair by the fireside. "I'll just have a little rest, and then I'll be on my way."

Soon he fell fast asleep and it was morning before Beauty's father awoke. "My daughters will be worried!" he cried, rushing outside to find his horse. Then, just as he was about to set off, he noticed an arch covered with the most beautiful roses he had ever seen. "At last–a red, red rose!" he cried, picking

the sweetest-smelling one for his youngest child.

"HOW DARE YOU STEAL MY ROSE!" roared an angry voice. "I gave you food! Is this how you repay me?" Beauty's father turned to face the owner of the house: A terrifying beast, dressed in the finest clothing. "I'm s…s… sorry!" said Beauty's father. "It was for one of my daughters."

"Then you must give me one of your daughters," replied the Beast harshly. "You must return with her by nightfall, or you will die!"

With a heavy heart, the old man set off for home once again. How could he give one of his daughters to such a creature? He would rather die! And that is what he told his girls when he arrived home.

Of course, Beauty refused to accept her father's judgement. "I cannot let you do this," she told him bravely.

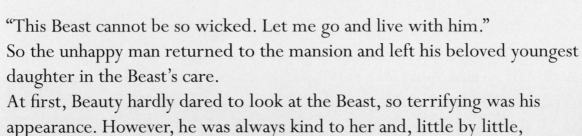

"This Beast cannot be so wicked. Let me go and live with him."
So the unhappy man returned to the mansion and left his beloved youngest daughter in the Beast's care.

At first, Beauty hardly dared to look at the Beast, so terrifying was his appearance. However, he was always kind to her and, little by little, Beauty began to understand him. Soon, she saw that beneath his terrifying appearance was a kind and generous heart.

"Why do you pretend to be so fearsome?" she asked him one night.
The Beast sighed heavily. "I know I frighten people," he confessed. "But how can I help that, looking like this? People expect the worst of me. That is why I shut myself away from the world."

One day Beauty and the Beast were strolling in the rose garden, when he took her hands in his. "Are you happy here with me?" he asked, looking deep into her eyes.

By now Beauty was no longer afraid
of the Beast's appearance. All she saw
was the kindness shining in his eyes.
"Yes," she answered honestly, "but I
miss my family."
The very next day, the Beast gave Beauty
a present.
"This is a magic mirror," he told her.
"When you look into it, you will see the
people you love."
Beauty was delighted. Now she could see
her father and sisters whenever she wanted.
But her joy did not last long. That night as she
gazed into the mirror, she saw her father lying
sick in bed. He looked old and worn.
"What's wrong?" asked the Beast, seeing Beauty's tears.
"My father is ill," she replied. "I am afraid he might die!"
The Beast sighed. "Go!" he told her with a heavy heart.
"But you must come back to me, or I, too, will die!"
Beauty threw her arms around the Beast and hugged
him. "Thank you for your kindness," she whispered.
"I'll never forget it. I promise I will return!"
The next day Beauty set off for home. Her father
was overjoyed when he saw his daughter. She was
the very person he longed to see! He knew that now she was home, he
would soon recover.
Days passed, then weeks, as Beauty cared for her father. But she never forgot
about the Beast.
"He may look fearsome, but he is the kindest and gentlest soul I have ever
met," she told her family.

One morning, when Beauty's father was well again, Beauty came across the magic mirror the Beast had given to her. Smiling, she picked it up and looked into it. Who would she see? There, gazing back at her was the face of the Beast. But he wasn't smiling–he looked very ill.

"My poor friend," she whispered, her heart filled with dread. "I have broken my promise! I must return to you!"

Beauty and her father set off for the mansion at once. There, they found the Beast lying lifeless in the garden by the rose arch.

Beauty took the Beast's hand in hers, and clasped it to her heart. Before she even knew what she was saying, words tumbled out of her mouth. "Please don't die," she cried. "I love you!"

As she spoke, something wonderful happened. The Beast opened his eyes and slowly sat up.

"My Beauty!" he smiled. Before her very eyes, the Beast's face began to change. He transformed into a handsome Prince.

"At last I am free!" he told Beauty, holding her hands in his. "Many years ago a witch put a wicked spell on me. Only true love could break it!"

The Prince plucked a single rose from the bush and held it out to Beauty. "Will you marry me?" he asked.

"It is all I desire," replied Beauty simply. "But you are a Prince, and I am just a poor girl and can give you nothing. You should marry a Princess."

The Prince shook his head. "What you have is far beyond riches and royalty," he told her. "I believed no one could ever love an ugly creature like me–but you saw into my heart and loved me for who I am."

"Then I shall marry you," cried Beauty, taking the rose. "It is all I desire!"

The Princess and the Peasant Girl

There was once a Princess named Isabella, who was tired of being royal and wished that she could be ordinary. The unhappy Princess could not dance very well, and hated attending balls. She got fed up making conversation with the boring dukes and princes that she met. She was uncomfortable in her gowns, because they were tight and stiff. She found it tiresome to sit still for hours while her portrait was painted. But, most of all, she hated the fact that she had to look pretty and behave herself all the time because everyone was always watching her. By coincidence, a girl named Isobel lived in a nearby village. She had been born on the same day as the Princess and she, too, was unhappy with her life. She was worn out from having to get up at dawn to feed the animals and draw water from the well. She was tired of spending the mornings helping her mother do the laundry and all the other household chores. She wished she could buy her clothes instead of having to make them. But, most of all, she hated the long, boring evenings when there was nothing to do but sew by the dim light of a candle, with only her family for company. Each day, Isobel longed to be a Princess and escape her difficult and dreary life.

One night, at exactly the same moment, just before they fell asleep, Isabella and Isobel both wished that they could change their lives forever. A good fairy heard the girls' wishes and was delighted that, with just one spell, she would be able to help two people at once.

"From their lives let each be free, and in each other's bodies be!" chanted the fairy and, with a wave of her magic wand, the spell was cast.

The next morning, Princess Isabella woke with a start. There was something wrong with her bed—it felt hard and lumpy. Then she heard a woman's voice calling her name, but it sounded odd, and it was even stranger for anyone to shout at her. When Isabella opened her eyes and looked around Isobel's simple bedroom with its bare wooden floor, she thought she must be dreaming.

The woman was still shouting, so the Princess thought she'd go see what was happening. She put on the worn dress that was hanging from a hook on the bedroom door and made her way downstairs in a daze.

"Hurry up," said Isobel's mother. "You have overslept. The animals are waiting for their food." The Princess stumbled outside. It didn't take her long to find the hungry pigs and hens, who were calling for their breakfast. The Princess fed them grain from a large barrel and went back indoors.

"Where's the water?" asked Isobel's mother.

The Princess had noticed a well in the yard, so she went out and drew a pail of water, just as she'd watched the servant boys in the palace kitchen gardens do. Isobel's mother gave her a strange look when she returned to the kitchen.

"I don't know what's the matter with you today, Isobel," she said. "You look as if you're still half-asleep."

That morning, the Princess followed Isobel's mother's instructions as if she were sleepwalking. After lunch, she had to run some errands in the village. As she walked down the lane to the shops, she remembered that she hadn't even looked in the mirror once. She had been so busy that morning, she hadn't given a thought to her appearance. She wondered what her subjects would say when they saw her wearing such a shabby dress, with her messy hair. But, to her great surprise, no one took any notice of her at all.

In the meantime, Isobel had woken up at the palace and she, too, noticed something strange about her bed. It was so soft, she felt as if she were floating on a cloud. She looked around the Princess's bedchamber in amazement, then sat bolt upright. The sun was already high in the sky—she should have fed the animals hours ago!

"Your breakfast, your Highness," said a maid, setting down a tray piled high with food and curtseying as she left. Completely bewildered, Isobel ate her breakfast. A lady-in-waiting arrived with a list of appointments and the day passed in a whirl of activity as everyone prepared for the Royal Ball that was being held at the palace that evening. When it was time to dress for the Ball, Isobel was overwhelmed by the Princess's sparkling jewels and exquisite ball gowns. She chose a beautiful, pink velvet dress with a ruby necklace and matching tiara. Happy that she would not have to get up at dawn the next day, Isobel stayed up later than ever before and danced until her feet ached. As she sank into her goosedown mattress that night, she felt as if all her dreams had come true.

The two girls settled into their new lives. Each afternoon, Isabella walked to the village, where she went about her business without being stared at all the time. She loved chatting with people and, for the first time in her life, she knew that they weren't being nice to her just because she was a Princess. She enjoyed the simple, fresh food eaten at the kitchen table with Isobel's large and cheerful family far more than the lonely meals in her royal apartment or the formal banquets, where her dresses were so tight she could hardly breathe, let alone eat. At the palace, Isobel took delight in her beautiful gowns and splendid surroundings. After years of looking after the animals and doing the household chores, she enjoyed having servants to take care of her every need. She adored going to balls and dancing all night, and she loved the attention of all the dukes and princes she met.

However, as time passed, the two girls became unhappy. The Princess grew tired of the household chores, which made her soft hands red and sore and, when winter came, she hated getting up in the cold and dark to feed the animals. To her surprise, she missed going to balls and wearing her beautiful gowns—even if they were a little uncomfortable at times. Isobel, meanwhile, missed her family and the animals she had cared for at home and, to her surprise, was bored doing nothing to help anyone else.

Filled with sadness, Isabella returned to the lake close to the palace, where she used to walk when she was a Princess. Isobel, too, was unhappy and lonely that day, because it was her mother's birthday, so she decided to go to the lake to be alone. As they walked around the lake in opposite directions, both girls started to cry. Blinded by their tears, they almost bumped into one another.

The good fairy was horrified to see that the two girls she had intended to help were so upset. She appeared at the lakeside just as they were explaining the reasons for their tears to one another.

The girls both admitted that, although they had longed for a different life, they now knew that they'd been happier before, so the fairy agreed to switch them back again.

The following morning, Isabella and Isobel woke up in their old beds, each pleased to be back where she belonged, and the two girls became the best of friends.

The Secret Princess

Once upon a time, in a kingdom far, far away, lived a beautiful Princess named Amelia. She was very pretty, with tumbling blond curls and large brown eyes. The Queen adored Princess Amelia and showed her daughter how to sing the sweetest songs, how to grow the prettiest flowers, and how to cook the tastiest soup. But, one day, there was great sadness in the palace. The Queen had died. Because the King loved Princess Amelia so much, he wanted only the best for her. He hunted throughout the land to find a new wife. Soon, the King announced he was to be married again.

"Now you've got a new mother," the King said happily to the Princess, after his wedding.

The Princess's new stepmother smiled coldly. As she gazed at her stepdaughter's youth and beauty, her heart burned with jealousy.

Early one morning, the stepmother woke Princess Amelia. She grabbed the Princess roughly by the arm and pulled her out of bed.

"You're coming with me," the stepmother hissed. "You will leave this kingdom and never return."

The Princess was taken to the stepmother's large country house. It was far away from anywhere, and the only people living there were servants, who weren't friendly. The stepmother took the Princess into the kitchens and dragged her to the cook.

"Amelia, you'll work as a kitchen maid," the Princess's stepmother said. "Cook will tell you what to do." And, with that, she strode out of the kitchen, leaving the Princess behind.

"Make some supper," Cook ordered.

"But I don't know how," the Princess protested. "All I can make is my mother's soup."

"Then make soup," Cook said, sinking down into a comfortable chair in front of the fire. "I've been working my fingers to the bone for years. Now it's your turn."

When the stepmother returned to the kingdom, she took the King aside.

"I'm afraid I have bad news. Your daughter has run away and she's nowhere to be found," she said.

The King was heartbroken. He did not know how he would live without his lovely daughter.

Once again, the palace was filled with sadness.

Many months passed. Princess Amelia's days were always the same. She'd wake early in her small, damp attic room and put on her gray, ragged servant's clothes. Then she would make soup, clean the kitchen, and sweep the house from top to bottom. Only after she'd finished all her jobs was she allowed into the garden, where she'd care for the flowers and plants that grew there. Being outside in the garden made the Princess happy and, when she was happy, she sang.

The Princess sang in the spring, as she tended to the bulbs and buds unfurled on the trees. She sang in the summer, as the flowers bloomed and the sun warmed her skin. She sang in the autumn, as the leaves changed their shades and fell to the ground. She even sang in the winter, as she cleared a blanket of snow from the earth.

One day, a Prince was passing by on his horse when he heard Princess Amelia's delightful voice singing a haunting melody. It was the sweetest sound he'd ever heard.

"The owner of such a voice must be incredibly beautiful," the Prince thought. "I must find out who she is!"

The Prince climbed down from his horse and peered through the hedge, trying to see who was singing. But the hedge was very thick, and the Prince could not see more than a glimpse of pink rags and a flash of blond hair.

The Prince rode up to the front of the house and knocked at the door. When Cook saw the Prince, her eyes widened with delight. She'd never met such a handsome man before.

"Good afternoon," the Prince said politely. "I've been traveling for many hours and was wondering if I could trouble you for something to eat?"

"Of course," Cook beamed. "I'll bring you some food immediately." When Cook returned, she placed a bowl of the Princess's soup in front of the Prince. The servants watched as he ate a spoonful then licked his lips.

"This is the best soup I've ever tasted," the Prince said. When the Prince had finished his meal, he sat back in his chair. "Who is the maiden singing in the garden?" he asked.

The servants all looked at each other. Their mistress had warned them they would be punished if they spoke to anyone about Princess Amelia.

"There's nobody in the garden," Cook lied.

"Yes, there is," the Prince said. "She has the most beautiful voice in the world. Won't you tell me who she is?"

"Sir, you are mistaken," Cook insisted. "There's nobody here but us. It must have been a bird singing."

Disappointed, the Prince left the house and rode away on his horse.

"You're forbidden to go outside anymore," Cook said to Princess Amelia. Instead, after the Princess had finished her chores, she was banished to the attic room. The Prince returned again and again to the house. Not only did he long for more of the delicious soup, he yearned to discover the identity of the maiden who'd sung so sweetly in the garden. But there was no sign of her and the Prince never heard the song again.

Although Princess Amelia was upset about being kept inside, she refused to feel sad. She was a kind and happy girl who enjoyed helping the other servants with their work. As more time passed, all of the servants, even Cook, grew to like Princess Amelia. One day, when the familiar knock on the door came, Cook entered the kitchen.

"Amelia, the Prince is waiting in the dining room," she said. "Why don't you take him his soup today?"

"Of course, Cook," the Princess said. She spooned the soup carefully into a bowl and sang as she carried it upstairs.

As the Prince heard the singing, his heart leaped. Finally, he would discover who had such a delightful voice! As Princess Amelia walked in, the Prince immediately fell in love. The girl was as lovely as her song.

"Please, won't you join me," the Prince said, as he took his soup.

As the Prince ate, they talked and talked. After the last drop of soup disappeared, the Prince took the Princess's hand in his.

"I wish to marry you," he said. "You are the most wonderful person I've ever met. But it seems fate is against us, for I can only marry the daughter of a King."

"But I am the daughter of a King!" Princess Amelia exclaimed with pleasure. She explained about her past and how she had been banished by her evil stepmother. The Prince was delighted. "In that case, we shall be married tomorrow," he declared. He took the Princess by the hand and whisked her away to his palace. The Prince informed Princess Amelia's father, who was joyfully reunited with his beloved daughter on her wedding day.

Soon, Princess Amelia had a large garden of her own to care for, and was so happy she sang all day for her husband, the Prince.

The Mysterious Maze

Once upon a time, there was a handsome Prince who lived in a magnificent palace with his father, the King. The Prince was gentle and kind, and was also very romantic. The King loved his son deeply, and longed for him to get married, but the Prince said he would only marry for love. The King was very worried about this, because if the Prince did not find a bride before his next birthday, he would not inherit the kingdom. Instead, it would go to the Prince's cousin, the Count, who was a cruel and arrogant man.

The King scoured the land and introduced his son to the loveliest maidens he could find. "I'm sorry, Father, but I'm still not in love," the Prince said. "I cannot marry any of them."

"Please, won't you reconsider?" the King asked in despair, for it was only a few days until the Prince's birthday.

"I believe in love at first sight," the Prince said. "I have not yet met the one I will spend the rest of my life with."

"But you will lose the kingdom if you don't find her soon," the King pleaded.

The Prince did not want the kingdom to go to his wicked cousin. But he knew he couldn't marry someone he didn't love. It was a tricky problem, and the Prince decided to go for a long walk to think about it.

The Prince walked through the palace gardens and into the woods. He thought for hours and still didn't know what to do. The Prince was about to return home when he heard the sound of barking.

"Bess, come back," a female voice called.

As the dog ran out from the trees, the Prince grabbed at its collar. He looked up to see a beautiful maiden running toward him. She had pale skin, long flowing hair, and big, blue eyes. The Prince's heart leapt and he knew instantly this was the girl he'd been waiting for.

"Thank you so much for catching her," the maiden said, smiling shyly. "I'm Lilly."

"I'm glad I could help," the Prince replied. He began talking to Lilly and, before long, it felt as though they'd known each other forever.

"I know this may be sudden, but I've loved you from the first moment I saw you," the Prince said, taking Lilly's hand. "Will you marry me and be my Princess?"

"Nothing would make me happier," Lilly said, blushing.

The Prince was delighted. "I can't wait to tell my father," he said. "Will you come to the palace tomorrow so he can meet you?"

"Of course," said Lilly.

They tenderly kissed good-bye and as the Prince made his way home, he was overjoyed.

Back at the palace, the Prince's cousin, the arrogant Count, and his mother, the Countess, had come to visit the King. The Countess could barely contain her excitement at the thought of her son ruling the land.

"Because your foolish child refuses to marry, it won't be long before the kingdom is ours," the Countess told the King nastily.

The King swallowed hard. He hated to think of the Count and Countess inheriting his palace.

"There's still time for the boy to find a bride," the King replied defiantly, as the Prince rushed into the Grand Hall.

"Indeed there is, and I have found her," the Prince said. "Father, I have finally fallen in love and we are to be married! Her name is Lilly and she will arrive here tomorrow, so you can meet her."

"What wonderful news," the King beamed, embracing his son.

The Count and Countess were furious, and stormed out of the palace.

"We must do everything we can to stop this wedding," hissed the Countess.

"That kingdom is mine," snarled the Count.

The Mysterious Maze

121

The two plotted and schemed, and eventually came up with a wicked plan. The Countess would disguise herself as an old woman, and trick Lilly into entering the palace maze, where she would be lost forever.

The next day, Lilly and her dog, Bess, approached the palace.

"Can you believe we're going to live here, Bess?" Lilly asked, excitedly. "It's a dream come true."

As Lilly walked toward the entrance of the palace, she saw an old woman, who appeared to be looking for something.

"Can I help you?" Lilly asked, approaching the woman.

"Oh, thank you so much," the Countess said, pulling her headscarf tightly around her face. "I've lost my ring and my eyesight is not very good."

"I'm sure we'll find it," Lilly said.

"I might have had it in there," the Countess said, pointing to the entrance of the palace maze.

The Countess led Lilly further and further into the maze. The Countess had taken care to learn the way out, so she wouldn't be lost herself. "Are you sure you lost your ring here?" Lilly asked nervously. The hedges of the maze were extremely high, and she was feeling very confused. "There is no ring, you foolish girl," the Countess said, throwing off her headscarf and revealing herself. "You've been tricked!" The Countess ran out of the maze, leaving Lilly and Bess alone. "What are we going to do, Bess?" Lilly asked in alarm. She desperately tried to find the exit, but every path she took was a dead end. Lilly turned left and right, but there seemed to be no escape. Finally, Lilly crumpled onto the ground and sobbed in despair.

"Now I'll never get married and become a Princess," Lilly cried, tears streaming down her face.

Just then, Lilly spotted a small gap at the bottom of the hedge. She was too big to fit through it, but Bess could!

123

"Come here, Bess," Lilly called. "You have to go through this gap and find the Prince. Tell him I'm here, do you understand?"

Bess barked and squeezed through the hole.

In the palace, the Prince was pacing back and forth nervously. Lilly was very late and he was worried.

"She's not here," the Countess sneered. "She's obviously changed her mind and doesn't want to marry you."

"The kingdom will be mine after all," the Count added, with a wicked smile.

It was then that a small white dog ran into the Great Hall and started barking.

"That's Lilly's dog!" the Prince exclaimed.

Bess ran over to the Prince and gently tugged at the leg of his pants.

"Has something happened to Lilly?" the Prince asked.

The dog ran outside and the Prince followed closely behind. Bess stopped at the maze entrance and began yapping furiously.

"Has Lilly gotten lost?" the Prince asked, going inside the maze and peering around the hedges. The Prince had been exploring the maze since he was a boy, so knew it well. Soon, he came across his true love, sitting on the ground where Bess had left her.

"I've finally found you," the Prince exclaimed happily, embracing Lilly. "We will be married tonight."

That evening, there was much rejoicing for the Prince and his glowing new bride, the rightful rulers of the kingdom, and the Count and Countess were never seen again.

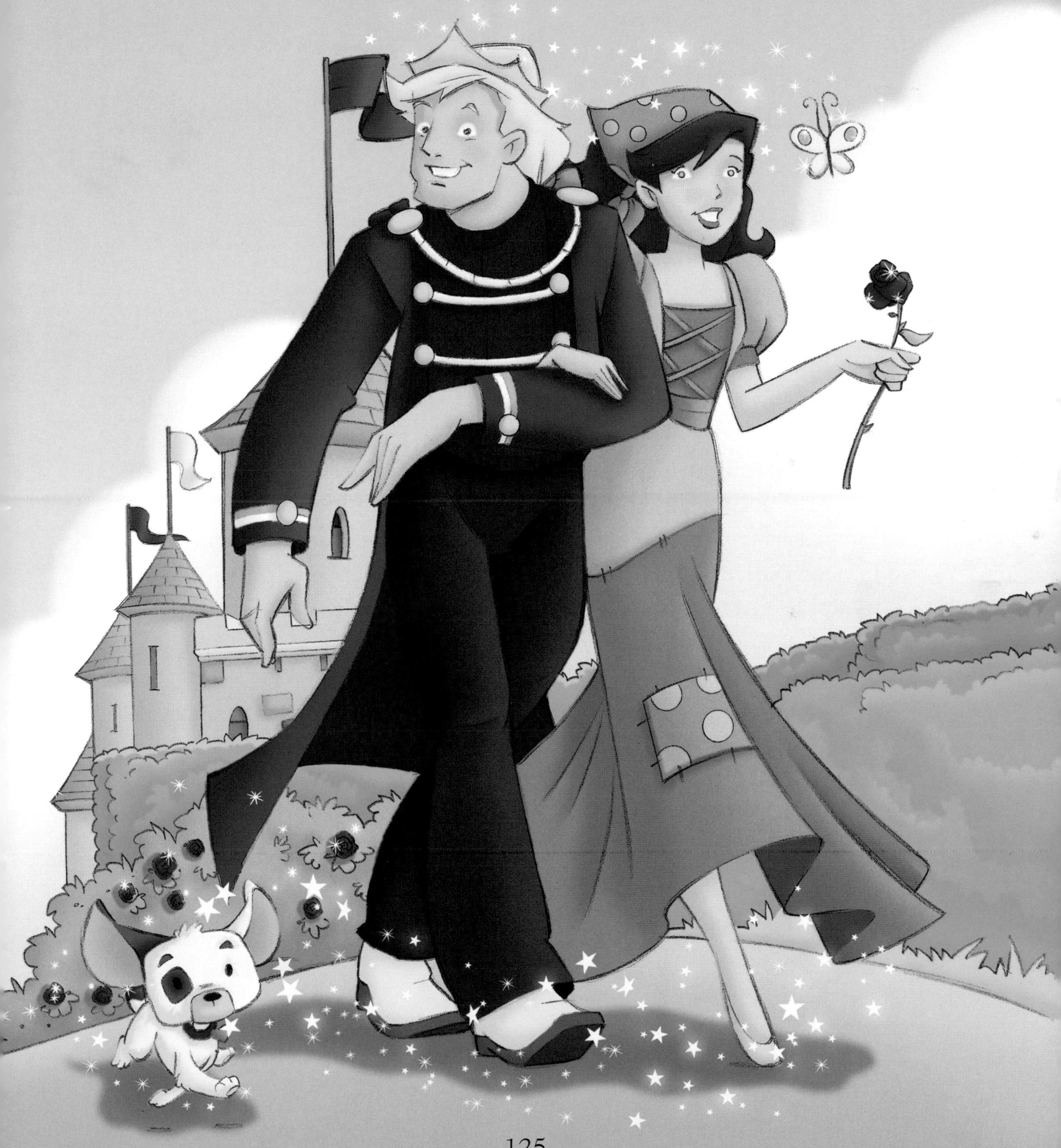

Rapunzel

Once upon a time, there lived a good man and his wife who were very unhappy because they had no children. The couple prayed that one day they would have a baby, and the wife felt sure that, in time, their wish would be granted.

Their little house overlooked a splendid garden, surrounded by a high wall, which was full of lovely flowers, herbs, and vegetables. But no one dared enter the garden because it was owned by a powerful witch, who was feared by all who knew her.

The wife often stood at her bedroom window, looking into the witch's garden, and one day she noticed a bed full of the most beautiful rapunzel leaves. They looked so fresh and green, she longed to make a salad of them. Each day, she gazed into the garden and all she could think about was eating the delicious leaves. Soon she lost interest in any other food and began to look quite pale and ill. Her husband was worried and asked her what was wrong.

"If I don't get some of those rapunzel leaves, I think I shall die," his wife replied. The man loved his wife so much that he was prepared do anything to make her well again, so that evening he climbed over the high wall into the witch's garden and quickly picked a handful of rapunzel leaves. He hurried back and gave them to his wife. She made them into a salad and they tasted so good, she immediately wanted some more. The following evening, just as it was getting dark, the man climbed the wall again to pick another bunch of rapunzel leaves for his wife. But when he jumped down into the garden he got a terrible shock—to his horror, he saw the old witch standing there waiting for him.

"How dare you climb into my garden like a thief and steal my rapunzel," she raged, her evil eyes blazing. "I'll make you pay for this!"

"I'm very sorry," said the man, shaking with fear. "I had no choice. My wife saw your rapunzel from her window and could think of nothing else. I'm sure she would have died if I hadn't picked some for her."

"Well, I will accept your excuse and make a deal with you," the witch said, after some thought. "You can take as much rapunzel as you like, but you must give me something in return. Your wife will soon give birth to a child. You must give the baby to me and I will care for it like a mother."

The man was so afraid that he agreed to do as the witch asked.

A week or two later, the man and his wife found they were expecting a child. When the woman gave birth to a daughter, the witch appeared and took the baby away. The couple were broken-hearted and cried for a year and a day. The witch named the child Rapunzel, after the salad leaves. Rapunzel grew into the most beautiful girl under the sun, with hair like spun gold.

When she was 12 years old, the witch took her deep into the forest and locked her in a room at the top of a tower. The tower had no door or staircase—just a tiny window right at the top. Whenever the witch wanted to enter, she called out, "Rapunzel, Rapunzel, let down your hair to me."

Then Rapunzel would let her long braids fall to the ground, so the witch could climb up them and come in through the window.

The witch visited the tower every day, but most of the time Rapunzel was alone, so she passed the long hours by singing to herself. At night, she dreamed of being rescued from her prison by a handsome Prince, who would make her his Princess and take her to live in a beautiful palace.

A few years later the King's son was riding through the forest and, as he approached the tower, he heard the most beautiful song. He stopped to listen, spellbound. He longed to see the owner of the lovely voice and looked for a door into the tower but there was none, so he gave up and rode home.

The young Prince couldn't forget the sound of Rapunzel's sweet singing so he returned every day, listening as her voice rang out into the forest. Then one day he saw the old witch approaching and hid behind a tree.

"Rapunzel, Rapunzel, let down your hair to me," cried the witch.

The Prince watched as Rapunzel let down her hair and the witch climbed up to the window.

"So that's the ladder into the tower," the Prince said to himself. The following day, as darkness fell, he rode to the tower and called out,

"Rapunzel, Rapunzel, let down your hair to me."

Rapunzel let down her hair, and the Prince climbed up to the window. Rapunzel was terribly frightened when he appeared, as she had never seen a man before, but the Prince explained that his heart had been so touched by her singing that he could not rest until he had seen her. He was so gentle and kind that she soon forgot her fear. The Prince visited each evening and one day he asked Rapunzel to marry him.

Rapunzel's heart leapt. At last she had a chance to escape from the tower and become a Princess, married to the man she loved. "I will gladly be your wife," she said. "But how will I get down from this tower?" Then she had an idea. "Each time you come to visit me, bring me a length of silk thread and I will weave a ladder so I can climb down. Then you can take me back to your kingdom."

The witch had no idea that the Prince had been coming to visit Rapunzel each evening until one day, when Rapunzel let down her hair for the witch to climb up, she said, without thinking, "Why is it that you are so much harder to pull up than the young Prince? He always climbs up in a moment."

"You wicked child!" shouted the witch. "I thought I had hidden you away from the world and now I find out that you have been deceiving me!" In a fury, she grabbed Rapunzel's hair and wrapped it around her left hand. She grabbed a pair of scissors with her right hand and, snip snap, she cut off all the long, golden hair. Then she took Rapunzel away to the wilderness and left her there.

Rapunzel

131

The witch returned to the tower and tied Rapunzel's hair to a hook inside the window. That evening, the Prince came as usual and called out, "Rapunzel, Rapunzel, let down your hair to me." The witch dropped the hair from the window and the Prince climbed up. But instead of finding his beloved Rapunzel at the top of the tower, he was greeted by the old witch.

"So, you thought you would find your true love here, but she is gone," cried the witch, fixing him with an evil stare. "Rapunzel is lost to you forever—you will never see her again."

Beside himself with grief and despair, the Prince threw himself from the tower and landed in a thorn bush. He escaped with his life, but the thorns scratched his eyes so badly that he could hardly see.

He stumbled through the forest, not knowing where he was going, miserable and weeping over the loss of his lovely bride. At last, he came upon the wilderness where Rapunzel was living. As he wandered through the bleak and lonely landscape, he heard a familiar voice singing a beautiful song. The Prince couldn't believe his ears and headed toward the sound. Although the young man looked different, Rapunzel

knew at once that it was him. During her years of misery, living alone in the wilderness, she had never forgotten her dream of marrying her true love and becoming a Princess. She threw her arms around his neck and wept with joy. Two of her tears fell into his scratched eyes, which healed immediately, so he could see just as well as before.

The Prince took Rapunzel back to his kingdom where they were welcomed with great joy. They were married and lived there happily ever after.

The Swan Princess

Once upon a time in a distant land, the King called his beautiful daughter, Odette, to him one day.

"When you came of age, it was your mother's dearest wish that you marry Prince Derek, son and heir to her oldest friend, Queen Uberta," he said. "That time has now come."

Odette was horrified. It was many years since she had seen Prince Derek–the little boy who pulled her hair and put frogs in her silk slippers.

"But Father," she cried. "I can't marry him. I would rather be locked in a tower!"

Her father smiled. "Prince Derek has grown into a fine young man," he said. "You will soon see for yourself as we have been invited on a royal visit."

Not far away, Prince Derek and his mother were discussing the marriage, too. "I can't marry that little cry baby!" laughed Prince Derek, thinking of the small girl he used to tease. "She looks like a scarecrow!"

Queen Uberta smiled. "Little girls grow up," she told him, wisely.

On the day of the royal visit Odette waited with her heart in her mouth as their coach rumbled toward Queen Uberta's palace—and the man she was supposed to marry.

A blast of royal trumpets announced their arrival, as a footman opened the coach door. Odette and her father stepped out into the sunshine. There to greet them was a tall young man with a charming smile. The two young people looked into each other's eyes shyly and blushed. It was love at first sight.

Soon the young couple was inseparable. All day long they walked and talked together, laughing at their childish memories and discovering more about each other. As each day went by, they fell more and more deeply in love.

The King and Queen Uberta were delighted with their matchmaking. "At last our two kingdoms will be united," they told each other.

But the path of true love does not always run smoothly. Though head over heels in love with Odette, Prince Derek was still young. When he finally plucked up courage to ask for her hand, he stuttered and stumbled so much that she became unsure.

"Tell me why you love me!" she begged him. "I need to know."

"You are so beautiful. . ." Derek told her, struggling to find the words.

"What else?" asked Odette, who wanted to be loved for herself, not her beauty.

"What else is there?" asked Prince Derek, unsure what to say.

Odette was furious. "I knew you were just a silly boy," she cried, as she stormed off. "I could never marry you."

The next day, the King and Princess Odette set off for home. "Won't you reconsider?" asked her father, as their carriage drew out of the palace gates.

But Odette was stubborn. She could not bring herself to forgive the Prince's thoughtless words–even though her heart ached for him.

As they rode back, the sky turned black and the air was filled with a cold wind. "This is the work of Rothbart," cried the King, fearing for his daughter's safety. Many years ago he had banished the evil enchanter from his kingdom. He knew the wicked villain would stop at nothing to gain revenge.

"Halt the coach and ride for help," he ordered his men.

Just then there was a loud crack of thunder and Rothbart appeared.

"I hear you want your daughter to marry!" sneered the evil enchanter, as he seized Princess Odette. "I have the perfect husband for her—ME!"

In a flash of light he disappeared, taking Odette with him.

The King was heartbroken by his loss, but no one was more devastated than Prince Derek.

"I will find Odette, no matter how long it takes," he vowed to her father.

For many months Prince Derek and his friend Bromley searched the kingdom for the missing Princess, but they could find no sign of her.

"I know you love her, but I fear she is gone forever," sighed his mother.

Prince Derek refused to listen. "I will not give up," he cried.

As he spoke, he looked up and saw a flock of graceful swans flying overhead. He watched as they came down to land on a nearby lake.

"Let's go hunting," suggested Bromley, anxious to distract his friend.

Though his heart was not in it, Prince Derek agreed. Together, they made their way down to the lake. Derek aimed his crossbow as a magnificent swan with snowy white feathers came down to land on the still water.

"Get ready. . ." he whispered under his breath. But just before he released the arrow, the beautiful white feathers melted away, and the swan changed into a young girl before his very eyes. It was Odette!

"I am trapped on this lake by Rothbart's wicked spell," the poor unfortunate girl told the Prince. "By night I am human, but by day I take on the form of a swan. Rothbart is determined to marry me, so he can take over my father's kingdom. I can never leave this place until the spell is broken."

"How can I break it?" asked the Prince. "Shall I kill Rothbart?"

"No, no!" cried Odette in alarm. "If Rothbart dies before the spell is broken, I will be trapped here forever. The enchantment can only be broken by a vow of everlasting love."

"I love you with all my heart!" cried Derek, seizing her hands.

"Then you must prove it to the world," Odette told him.

Prince Derek thought for a moment. "Tomorrow night a ball is to be held," he said. "I will declare my love for you before the whole court!"

As Prince Derek left, Rothbart appeared on the banks of the lake.

"So you think you can outwit me!" he muttered. "Just you wait. . ."

On the night of the Birthday Ball, Prince Derek waited anxiously on the steps of the palace. He could think of nothing and no one but Odette. His heart leapt as he saw her beautiful smiling face in the crowds. She had come! Running forward, he clasped her by the hands.

"Come with me," he cried joyously. "I want the whole world to know how I feel."

He was too excited to notice Rothbart lurking in the crowd.

Prince Derek held up his hands for silence.

"I have a wonderful announcement to make," he began.

At that very moment, he caught sight of a beautiful face in the crowd. It was Odette. But how could it be? She was standing beside him.

"Go on, make your vow!" sneered an evil voice behind him. "But make sure you choose the right girl, or the real Odette will die!"

It was Rothbart! He had used his wicked magic to disguise his own daughter as Odette. Now there were two Odettes!

How was Prince Derek to tell the difference?

"Odette!" he cried to the girl in the crowd. "Is that you?" But Rothbart had put a spell of silence on her, so she couldn't speak.

Prince Derek looked at each girl. Both had a freshness and beauty that made his heart ache. But he knew now there was more to Odette than her just her beauty. He looked deep into the eyes of both girls, then spoke.

"My Odette is brave and kind and generous," he cried, "and she loves me with all her heart. I can see it in her eyes."

Then he took the hands of the real Odette in his. "This is the girl I want to marry!"

As he spoke, there was a bright flash of light as Rothbart and his daughter disappeared forever. At last the evil spell was broken!

Odette threw herself into the Prince's arms. "Your words were beautiful," she told him. "Now I see that you love me for what is on the inside, not just for my beauty. Of course I will marry you!"

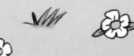

The Ice Kingdom

Once upon a time, there was a good, kind Prince who lived in a sunny land, filled with warmth and joy. He was betrothed to a beautiful young woman, but he soon discovered that she had a cold and cruel heart. When the hens stopped laying, she threw a plate at her maid because there were no eggs for breakfast. When a dog ran across her path, she tried to kick the poor animal, so it ran away howling. The Prince decided that he could not marry such an unkind girl, so he broke off their engagement.

When the young woman heard the news, she flew into a rage. Slowly, her lovely face changed—her button nose grew long and pointed, her full red lips became thin and pale, her smooth skin wrinkled, and her warm brown eyes turned cold and black. She was really an evil sorceress who had disguised herself as a beautiful girl so she could marry the Prince and steal his wealth. In her fury, she cast a spell over the Prince and his kingdom:

"Let sun be gone and cold winds blow.
Cover the kingdom with ice and snow.
Rid this land of all good cheer.
And freeze the hearts of those who live here."

As the sorceress left, a thick fog wrapped itself around the palace and spread throughout the land, blocking out the sunlight. When the fog lifted, a blizzard raged and the kingdom was blanketed in snow for the first time that anyone

could remember. The golden fields of corn, the green pastures, and the bright wildflower meadows were now completely white. The birds and butterflies had flown away, soon followed by all the other animals.

The ground was too cold to grow food, so the people were forced to live on a diet of gruel and pickled cabbage.

The Prince, once so happy and generous, became as bitter and cold-hearted as the sorceress, and his hungry subjects soon turned as frosty as the weather. News of the gloomy ice kingdom spread far and wide, and no one wanted to visit the freezing land or its miserable people.

One day, a Princess was going to visit her cousin, and her path went close to the ice kingdom. The journey had taken longer than expected and it was growing dark. The horses were tired, so the Princess and her servants decided to stop for the night. In the distance, they spotted a palace looming out of the icy mist, so they made their way toward it. As they approached, the air became colder and colder, and soon the horses' warm breath was billowing around the carriage

144

like smoke. When they reached the palace, it was dark and silent. They knocked loudly on the front door. Finally, the hinges—which had remained closed for years—creaked and squealed, as a palace footman forced it open.

He reluctantly let them in and took them to see the Prince.

"I'm sorry to disturb you, your Royal Highness," the Princess began politely. "We have been on the road all day and still have far to go. Would you be so kind as to let us rest here for the night?"

It had been many years since the Prince had received visitors and he was tempted to send the Princess away. But there was something about her bright and friendly nature that reminded him of happier times, so he allowed the group to stay for just one night.

That evening, the Princess entertained everyone by playing the piano and singing in her sweet voice. It was the first time music had been heard in the kingdom since it fell under the sorceress's spell and, gradually, people began tapping their feet, while some even hummed along.

Later, the Prince awoke to a strange sound. He was sure he could hear something dripping, but he thought he must be dreaming and went back to sleep.

But when he looked out his window the next morning, he saw that the icicles hanging from the palace roof were melting, and patches of green grass were appearing through the thick carpet of snow.

The Princess's coachmen went to prepare the horses for their departure, but one horse was lame. "It was so kind of your Royal Highness to allow us to stay here last night," the Princess said to the Prince. "Unfortunately one of our horses is lame. May we stay a little longer so he can recover?"

To his surprise, the Prince found that he was glad the Princess would not be leaving, and quickly agreed. The Prince and Princess spent the day together and the servants were shocked to hear the unusual sound of laughter echoing through the palace.

The next morning, the Prince awoke to another strange noise. It took him a while to think what it might be. Suddenly he remembered—it was birdsong! Then, when he opened his eyes, he noticed that his bed chamber was brighter than usual. The sun was shining! Looking out the window, he saw that the fields were now more green than white. Only a few small patches of snow remained. The sorceress soon heard that the frozen land was warming up, and she hurried there immediately to find out why the kingdom was no longer in her icy grip. As soon as she saw the Princess, the evil witch knew that the girl's warm and sunny nature had broken the spell. The sorceress decided that the only way to bring back the snow and ice was to cast a spell on the Princess too, so she disguised herself as an old woman and approached the girl in the palace gardens.

"Hello, my dear," said the sorceress. "May I walk with you?"

"Of course. Why don't you take my arm?" the Princess offered, kindly.

"The path is still a little icy in places and I wouldn't want you to slip." As they walked through the abandoned rose garden, the sorceress tried to cast an evil spell on the cheerful girl and turn her heart to ice, but the Princess just carried on making pleasant conversation.

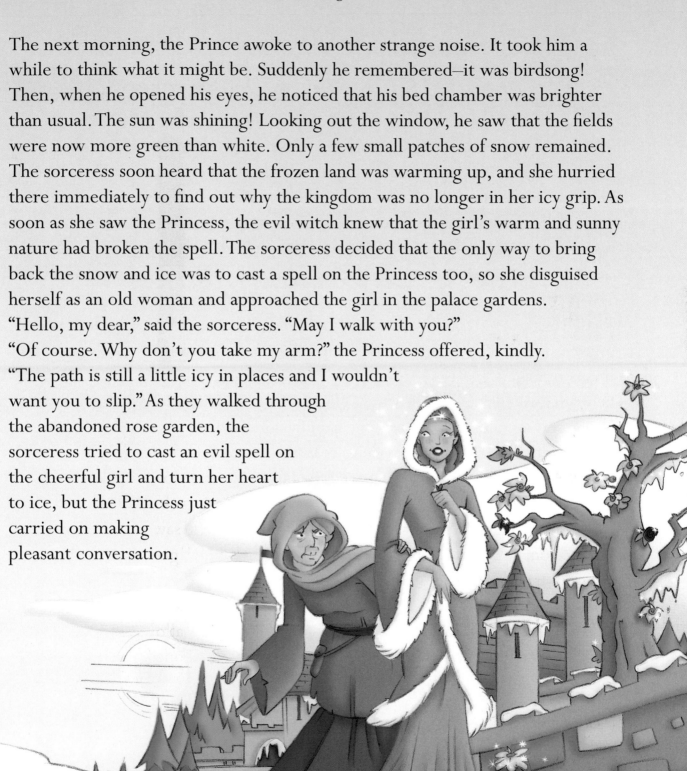

147

"Are you warm enough?" she asked the old woman. "If not, I will happily lend you my shawl."

Summoning all her powers, the sorceress tried one last time to cast her wicked spell and make the warm-hearted girl cold and sad. This time the spell worked, but not in the way the witch had intended. The magic bounced off the kind and friendly Princess and struck the sorceress instead, turning her to solid ice. The Princess was shocked to find that the old woman who had been walking alongside her a moment ago was now a frozen statue.

The sorceress was powerless and the kingdom was free of her evil magic. It wasn't long before all the snow and ice disappeared and everyone was outside enjoying the warm sunshine. People began chatting to one another again and whistled as they repaired their houses and tended their gardens. Children played games in the meadows, farmers replanted their crops, flowers bloomed, and the animals returned.

The Prince asked the kind-hearted Princess if she would be his wife and, now that she had seen his true nature, she happily agreed. Everyone in the kingdom was invited to a party at the palace to celebrate the royal engagement. There was much laughter and merry-making, as if the guests were trying to make up for their many years of sadness.

Although the kingdom was warm and sunny once more, there was one small corner of the palace garden that remained forever cold. Hidden among the bright red and yellow roses was the icy figure of the sorceress.

"This frozen statue will remain here forever to remind us that happiness is far more important than all the wealth in all the kingdoms in the world," the Prince told his joyful people.

The Mermaid Princess

In the deepest part of the ocean, where the water is coolest and calmest, stood the palace of the Sea King. The Sea King lived with his six daughters.
The youngest of the six Princesses, Ruby, was the loveliest, for not only was she beautiful, she was as kind and good as anyone could be. Ruby loved nothing more than listening to the stories her grandmother told about life above the sea. "On your next birthday," her grandmother told her, "you will be old enough to go to the surface."

Finally, Ruby's birthday arrived. She woke up full of excitement that today she would be allowed to go to the surface and, as soon as she could, she went to find out what life above the waves was like. Up and up she swam, until she felt the cool air all around her.
The sun had gone down, but thousands of bright stars twinkled in the ink-blue sky. It was the most wonderful sight Ruby had ever seen. Just when she thought nothing could be prettier, a great ship appeared.

It was covered in lights that were all the shades of the rainbow. Music and laughter sounded all around as the passengers celebrated and sang happy birthday to a young Prince.

Ruby swam closer and saw the Prince, who was very handsome, and Ruby imagined what it would be like to dance with him.

Suddenly, enormous storm clouds rolled across the sky, hiding the stars, and the waves grew larger, hitting the ship like huge black mountains. The whole ship creaked and groaned until one huge wave tipped it over and water began to rush over its sides.

As people rushed to the lifeboats, Ruby saw the Prince fall into the rough sea. He tried to swim but his arms soon became tired. The Prince began to sink. Ruby knew that she must save him and swam against the fierce waves to reach him. She helped the Prince keep his head above water and allowed the waves to carry them to shore.

It was morning when the sea finally brought Ruby and the Prince to shore. Ruby stayed with the Prince for as long as she could, singing softly to him and letting the sun dry his wet clothes. It was only when she heard voices approaching that she returned to the water and swam back to her home beneath the waves.

As the days became weeks, and then months, Ruby found herself thinking more and more about the Prince. She often swam to the spot where she had left him, hoping to see him again, but she never did.

"How I wish I could speak to him," Ruby sighed. "If only I were human. . ."

"But you can be, my dear," a voice spoke to her.

Princess Ruby turned toward the voice and saw that the Sea Witch had found her.

"I can grant your wish," the Sea Witch told her. "Then you could find your Prince."

Ruby hesitated, her father had always told Ruby to stay away from the Sea Witch, but she longed to see her Prince again, so she agreed.

"Swim to the shore before sunrise and drink this potion. It will make you human and turn your tail into legs," said the Sea Witch, handing Ruby a violet bottle. "If the Prince falls in love with you, you can stay human forever."

Ruby was delighted.

"However," added the Sea Witch, "if he does not love you by the time the sun sets on the second day, you will become a mermaid again and you must serve me for the rest of your life. In exchange for all this, I will need something from you." The Sea Witch paused to think. "I will need your beautiful voice."

Ruby nodded her agreement, but let out a final cry as she felt her lovely voice disappear. Ruby swam to the shore, curled up on the sand where she had left the

Prince, and drank the purple potion. A strange tingling started in her legs and, as Ruby watched, her shimmering tail became a pair of legs, with toes that she could wiggle in the sand.

In the castle nearby, the Prince was staring out toward the beach, and the sea beyond, hoping to hear the gentle song of the girl who had save his life. He could not remember her face, or her name, but her singing voice was the most wonderful sound he had ever heard.

Suddenly, he saw a young girl on the beach. She was dripping wet, as if she had just stumbled out of the ocean. At once, he sent a servant to fetch the girl, take her into the palace, and make sure she was cared for.

"You are very familiar to me," the Prince told her as she sat next to him at the Royal Banquet table that night. "I feel I know you, but I don't know how." Unable to answer him, Princess Ruby just smiled. But her smile did not last long, because she soon heard that a Princess, whom the King and Queen wanted the Prince to marry, was arriving the next day. Ruby thought that her heart might break. Not only would she lose her Prince, she would have to return to the sea and serve the Sea Witch, never seeing her family again.

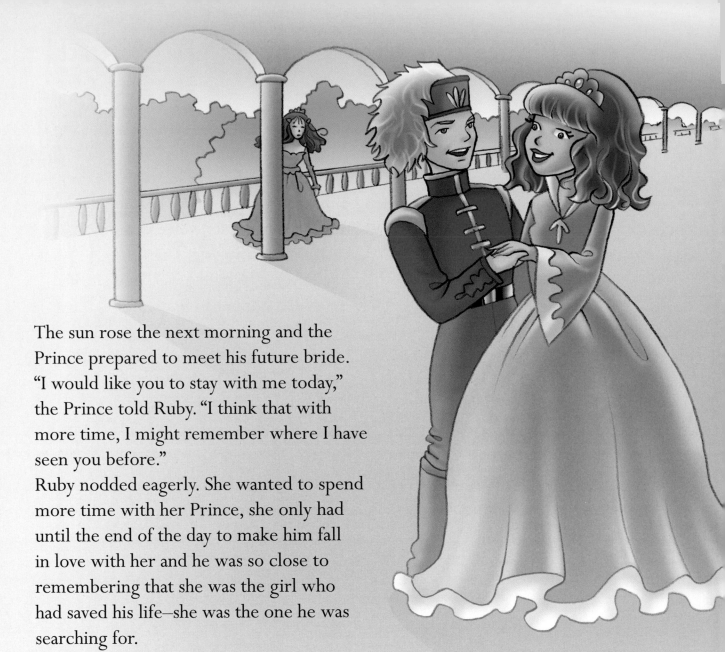

The sun rose the next morning and the
Prince prepared to meet his future bride.
"I would like you to stay with me today,"
the Prince told Ruby. "I think that with
more time, I might remember where I have
seen you before."

Ruby nodded eagerly. She wanted to spend
more time with her Prince, she only had
until the end of the day to make him fall
in love with her and he was so close to
remembering that she was the girl who
had saved his life—she was the one he was
searching for.

The Princess arrived and was shown into the courtyard. The happiness Ruby
had felt just moments before was soon gone because the Princess was the most
beautiful girl Ruby had ever seen. She had long, dark hair that fell in ringlets to
her shoulders, big eyes that were a perfect blend of green and brown, and her
cheeks were as rosy as ripe apples against her snow-white skin. There was no way
that the Prince could not love her. Trying to fight the tears in her eyes, Ruby ran
from the courtyard and to her room where she cried with silent sobs.

Princess Ruby was stirred from her sadness by a knock at her door. Cautiously, she opened it, to find the Prince standing on the other side.

"I cannot marry the Princess," he told her.

Ruby wiped her face.

"When I saw you run from the courtyard with tears in your eyes I knew that it was you I loved," the Prince confided. "I have been searching for months for a girl I thought I might never find. She saved my life and all I can remember is her voice. I will not let a second girl go."

Then he leaned closer to Ruby and kissed her.

At once, the Sea Witch's spell was broken and Ruby's voice returned to her. She was so happy that she began to sing.

"It's you!" said the Prince. "You were the girl who saved me. That is where I know you from." He picked Ruby up in his arms and embraced her. "You are the one I have been searching for and it is you I wish to marry."

Princess Ruby and the Prince were married on a beautiful ship in the middle of the ocean. Guests at the wedding said that a school of dolphins watched the whole service, but Ruby knew that it was her family celebrating her wedding and that her wish had come true–Ruby would live happily ever after with her Prince.

The Riddle

Once upon a time, in a kingdom faraway, lived a King and his children. He had three sons, the Princes, and a daughter, the Princess. Although the King loved all of his children dearly, his sons were very spoiled and foolish, and the King had little hope for them. However, his only daughter was a joy. She studied hard and always paid attention to everything the King taught her. While the Princes were playing hide-and-seek in the palace grounds, the Princess would be in the library, reading.

One day, the King was riding his horse through the fields when he was kidnapped by a dragon, who imprisoned the King in his cave.

When the horse returned to the palace without the King, a search party was sent out to find him. After many nights, they found the dragon's cave.

"You must release the King!" ordered the leader of the search party.

"Not until a riddle is solved," the dragon replied. The dragon was very cunning, and loved riddles, as all dragons do.

The search party returned to the palace and told the Princes what the dragon had said.

156

The eldest Prince stood up. "I'll go," he said. "I'm sure I can easily answer any riddle the dragon can give me."

The Prince saddled up his horse and rode to the cave. "Dragon, are you there?" he called.

"I demand you free the King immediately," the Prince ordered.

"You will have to solve a riddle first," the dragon said. "Listen carefully. I can run but never walk, have a mouth but never talk, have a head but never weep, have a bed but never sleep. What am I?"

The Prince thought for a long time, but had no idea what the answer might be.

"A tree?" the Prince said, eventually.

"You're wrong," laughed the dragon with delight. "I won't release your father."

So the eldest Prince returned to the palace without the King.

The middle Prince saddled up his horse and rode to the cave. "Dragon, are you there?" he called.

"I demand you free the King immediately," the Prince ordered.

"You will have to solve a riddle first," the dragon said. "Listen carefully. Give me food and I will live; give me water and I will die. What am I?"

The Prince thought for a long time, but had no idea what the answer might be. "A camel?" the Prince said, eventually.

"You're wrong," laughed the dragon with delight. "I won't release your father." So the middle Prince returned to the palace without the King.

Then the youngest Prince saddled up his horse and rode to the cave. "Dragon, are you there?" he called.

"I demand you free the King immediately," the Prince ordered.

"You will have to answer a solve first," the dragon said. "Listen carefully. I come at night without being called and am lost in the day without being stolen. What am I?"

The Prince scratched his head. He thought and thought, but had no idea what the answer might be.

"A robber?" the Prince said, eventually.

"You're wrong," laughed the dragon with delight. "I won't release your father." So the youngest Prince returned to the palace without the King.

"What are we going to do?" the Princes asked each other in despair. "If we can't solve the dragon's riddles our father will be a prisoner forever."

"I'd like to go see the dragon," the Princess said.

"Don't be so silly," the Princes laughed. "You won't be able to solve the puzzles. They're far too difficult."

"I'd like to try," the Princess said.

The Princes looked at each other and shrugged.

The Princess saddled up her horse and rode to the cave. "Dragon, are you there?" she called.

When the dragon saw the Princess, he smirked.

"I'd like to answer a riddle," the Princess told the dragon.

"I've given your brothers many chances," said the dragon, "so you will have to solve all my riddles in order to free the King. Listen carefully. I can run but never walk, have a mouth but never talk, have a head but never weep, have a bed but never sleep. What am I?"

The Princess thought hard, and looked around. In the valley below, she watched two children playing in a stream, and then the answer came to her. "A river," she said.

The dragon frowned. "That is correct," he said, annoyed. "But you will never solve my next riddle. Give me food and I will live; give me water and I will die. What am I?"

The Princess thought hard, and looked around again. On a faraway hillside, she could see a plume of smoke coming from a chimney. The answer came to her. "Fire," she said.

The dragon frowned and stamped one foot. "That is correct," he said. "But you will never guess my third and final riddle. I come at night without being called, and am lost in the day without being stolen. What am I?"

The Princess thought hard, but didn't know the answer. However, she was desperate to free her father, so she refused to be defeated. The Princess sat down nearby to try to solve the puzzle. Eventually, night fell. The Princess gazed up at the sky, and suddenly she jumped to her feet and ran to the cave's entrance. "Stars!" the Princess called to the dragon.

The dragon was furious. He hadn't expected the Princess to solve his riddles. But she had answered all three correct, so he couldn't go back on his word. The dragon called for the King, and told him he was no longer a prisoner.

"Which of my children has freed me?" the King said. He smiled when he saw the Princess and hugged her. "I thought it would be you, my beautiful, clever daughter, who listened to everything I ever taught her," he said proudly. "Thank you."